The Crossover Girl & Other Stories

The Crossover Girl & Other Stories

Ashok Ahlawat

Title: The Crossover Girl & Other Stories
Author: Ashok Ahlawat

ISBN: 978-93-92210-22-8

Edition: I

Published by:
J.G.S. Enterprises Pvt Ltd
Imprint: The Browser

Publisher's Address:
SCO 14-15, FF, Sector 8-C, Chandigarh 160 009

Website: www.thebrowser.org
Email: service@thebrowser.org

Editing, Layout and Cover Design by 99 beagles
www.99beagles.com

Disclaimer:
All names, characters, and incidents portrayed in this work are fictitious. No identification with actual persons (living or deceased), places, buildings, and products is intended or should be inferred.

www.thebrowser.org
Publishers & Booksellers

www.faujidays.com
Oral History and Military Publishing

I know more than I can express in words, and
the little I can express would not have been expressed,
had I not known more.
—Vladimir Nabokov

~

In the loving memory of my dear father
who laid out the tar on the roads of my mind.

Contents

Foreword

I was delighted to receive and read the book *The Crossover Girl & Other Stories* by Colonel Ashok Ahlawat. Anyone who has been in the Armed Forces and lived in far-flung areas of India with its varied and demanding terrain carries within a host of funny, poignant, and sometimes sombre memories that are shared only with a band of brothers that have been a part of them. These stories, unfortunately, are seldom shared with the public at large, who remain oblivious to the joys, adventures, challenges, and, at times, sadness of life in the Army.

The Crossover Girl & Other Stories is a collection of brilliant storytelling by an author who is observant, sees humour in difficult situations, and is brutally honest. Rudyard Kipling had stories and poems to write about the Army of the Raj, and now, we have a lad with an institutional memory of generations of soldiers and officers that followed the drum from his village, Gochhi, to lead us through Army cantonments, battalions, regiments, brigades, divisions and battlefields, mountains, deserts, and also to discover why a leopard died of shame!

I hope this book is read widely and it does indeed 'crossover' abroad to inform readers that the Indian Army continues to march on to the drum of courage.

—Lieutenant General TS Shergill, PVSM

Praise for the Author

~

A few years ago, I received a call, and it seemed a young aspiring writer was very keen to meet me. I have published novels, plays and many books for children...so it happens sometimes, and I thought it was one of those times. I asked him to come over to my home.

When I met Ashok, he appeared like any ordinary officer from Haryana that I had encountered in my life as an Army daughter and wife.

He belonged to Gochhi, my husband's village, one of the most notorious villages in Haryana. We shared a surname besides the love of reading and writing. However, I could never have guessed the talent that lay cached in the quill of this young man. He began forwarding me some anecdotes and tales he had written and was writing. His articles were published in newspapers. The more I read, the more I realised—this man had an extraordinary gift.

Ashok Ahlawat's pen weaves a wily magic. His descriptions of landscape and terrain and the use of metaphor and simile are unparalleled. He leads the reader into a world at once familiar to many yet unknown in the perspective he brings to it. A perspective that can enthral you with the way it perceives beauty, still your heart with compassion, and sadden you with its acuity.

Ashok understands the different kinds of cultures that can be found in India, and he manages to romance rusticity with such sophistication of thought and language that it makes one catch one's breath. And he brings all the adventure, romance, hardship, and devotion of a soldier's life right into yours.

The characters in his short stories actually exist as people—not merely as pawns who serve a writer's intent, and these are many, for the stories are set in varied locales and times—from the present to the past. These are true stories deftly told, braided with the perceptiveness of the writer, into a near-cinematic experience for the reader.

I expect to read many more insightful tales written by Ashok, and I feel certain his work will one day be critically acclaimed.

—Mariam Karim-Ahlawat, Author
My Little Boat and *The Street of Mists*

Author's Note

~

Life in the Army is not always pulsing with a light on your nose tip and the gentle kiss of excitement. In fact, boredom, like desert sand, is a long partner in any soldier's life. Long, unbroken stretches of disciplined monotony keep shaking hands. After many kind years in the Army, I have picked up the old furniture of life and laid it out as stories in this book.

As Joseph Conrad said, reality, as usual, beats fiction out of sight. I remember two days of my life clearly. The first is the day I walked to my village school with a writing planchette washed with Fuller's earth, a Reed pen, and an inkwell of tin that had a blue-coloured rubber cork. The second day I remember is the day I picked up a big rupee coin with wheat stalks and the numeral '1' embossed on it and bought a pen. I was not authorised to spend that rupee. I had to return that pen and give the rupee back to my father. But the journey of my familiarity with the pen had commenced.

I have always felt great joy whenever I read a good story or a good book. My father had books in tin trunks that we carried from station to station. I ended up reading all his books in childhood and hoped that one day, I would also write. This is my work. These are the purest words I have—I show them to you as friends show each other treasure stones.

I knew that the seed of literary endeavour had already been planted in the soil of my head. But one can't just sit and start writing without living a life. One can become a journalist, report, create content, and all that, but good and honest writing—well, that takes time. I didn't want to start writing with half-baked ideas. Not to mention, I was also an Army officer with a family who had heavy calls on my time and energy. But by and by, I got on with reading the authors I had chosen to read—after the house slept in the still majesty of dark nights and read till midnight.

One day, while I was sitting in the office, I saw messages floating on WhatsApp about the grisly murder of an Army officer's wife by her paramour. It was such a dreadful tragedy; such a beautiful life so cruelly extinguished. I still remember the date—23 June 2018. I picked up my pen, imagined the whole episode happening, and wrote a fictional story based on the murder.

I feel like that was my 'eureka' moment. After that day, I started writing. Mentally, I wanted to measure up to the sublime prose of Hardy, Lawrence, and Conrad.

Writing, after all, is like a glow worm—wringing the steps of darkness into light with the gentle scratch of pen on paper, and I was but a small creature with a dim torch in the immensity of the universe.

I am profusely thankful to Lieutenant General Maun Shergill for connecting me to Mr Pankaj P Singh of *The Browser* and *Fauji Days*. Without a good publishing house, all good writing is roofless. I am also most indebted to my editor, Alisha Verma, and her entire team, who weeded the text and cleaned it of mistakes and errors. Theirs was a tough task, and they did it superbly.

Raisins and Almonds

Ferozepur was a cantonment of numerous long Raj-era barracks. There was nothing much to look at in Ferozepur except the Saragarhi Gurudwara, the few war memorials on the Mall Road, the old church, and a low-walled star fort built by the East India Company. The star fort was used to house their furthermost arsenal before they had captured Maharaja Ranjit Singh's territory north of the Satluj *darya*. The Sikhs gave the East India Company permission to go through their territory to invade Afghanistan in 1839, and that's when Ferozepur became the northernmost bastion of the British Empire. After Partition, the Radcliffe Line ran just ten kilometres north of Ferozepur.

My father's Regiment, 20th Lancers, was stationed at Ferozepur when I must have been around 12 years old. We were studying in a school there. In those days, government transport department buses did not charge any bus fare from students. Some of us boys from the families of 20th Lancers decided that we should visit the Samadhi Memorials of Shaheed Bhagat

Singh and Sukhdev, which were located not very far off at Kaisar-e-Hind Bridge on the Satluj.

The roadways bus dropped us short of Hussainiwalla. We walked across the Satluj, peering into the water that carried a lot of tangled water hyacinths, *singhada* plants, and water lilies.

We walked across the watering tower of the Kaisar-e-Hind Bridge, saw the memorials of Shaheed Bhagat Singh and Sukhdev, loitered around, and started walking on a nice track westward.

'Let's see what lies up ahead!' someone shouted.

'Oh yes, why not? Let's walk up to Lahore and back!' one of the boys threw another gauntlet. So, we had a new purpose: to see the fabled city of Punjab and Maharaja Ranjit Singh. All of us started jogging and trotting, thinking that we would soon reach Lahore.

About a mile ahead, we ran into tall men in black salwar kameez with peaked turbans. They saw this group of *chokras* and halted us, *'Baccha log, kidhar jaata hai?'* (Children, where are you headed to?)

'Sir, we are headed for Lahore. We want to see the great city of India. Our grandparents have spoken so much about Lahore,' I replied.

The tall Pakistani ranger asked, '*Tum konsey zilley se ho?*' (Which district do you belong to?)

I told him I was from Rohtak *zila* (district). In fact, most of us belonged to the Rohtak area. The man in the *turrey wala safaa* took us to their barrack and gave us raisins, pistachios, and almonds.

'*Bachha log, khao*,' (Children, eat) he said.

So, we ate some dry fruits and stood looking at the tall men, wondering what they would do next. One of them went to a magneto phone and spoke to someone. Then, he turned towards us and smiled, saying, '*Baccha log*, fill up all your pockets with as many raisins and pistachios as you can.'

So, we stuffed our pockets full of pistachios and then picked up as many as our hands could hold. Then, the tall men asked us to follow them. We walked back all the way towards Ferozepur. At one place, one of the tall men stood and blew a whistle. An Indian soldier emerged some distance away.

This man shouted, '*Tumhara baccha log idhar aa gaya hai.* (Your kids have come to this side.) Come and take them away.'

An Indian Jeep came, and we were brought back to 20th Lancers. The Commandant was in his office. My father was a Head Clerk. He started thrashing us boys, and soon, the office floor was littered with raisins and pistachios.

The Commanding Officer (CO), Colonel Rajinder Singh, was watching everything from the office. He shouted, '*Arey* Subbey Singh, why are you beating these boys black and blue?'

Hearing the CO, my father stopped thrashing us. The Colonel waved at us and called us to his office. He heard our story and smiled at us. He gave us each a pencil and a foot rule. He then said to us, 'Don't go there again, boys.'

But the sobering effects of our thrashings and the CO's kind words wore off after a few days, and we were again up to making mischief.

An NDA Boy

I knew that in that stern Shaolin Monastery, and possibly for many long years thereafter, I wouldn't be able to keep long hair. The Army welcomes many kinds of weird boys into their officer factory. The welcome is more of an unwelcome.

I remember that I was wearing my favourite jeans, stitched at Mohan Singh in Delhi, and a white shirt. I was quite a Delhi cad in sartorial perfection. I had six-inch tresses, long sideburns, and an unfertile upper lip. The dulcet chin and the virgin territory between the nose and the lip were smooth as lavender.

There was never a scintilla of doubt in my mind that I would join National Defence Academy (NDA). The reason was my father—a big mustachioed infantryman—an officer of heavy self-respect and *izzat;* a tough guy, real man, an honourable old breed who never sucked up to anyone. His word was his bond. A gallantry awardee of genuine valour, he was a kind man and a good *fauji* father who kicked open the doors of life. I would thank him forever.

The train stopped at Pune. There were soft *taant*[1] voices all around. My leather ears were accustomed to the gruff, blunt cadences of Haryanvi. On the other hand, there were stalls selling buns and potato stuffing in polite Marathi. The drill *ustads* in the station portico had clipboards, and the eagle sword anchor crest of the NDA emblazoned on a maroon wooden board.

We dragged our black trunks into a Shaktiman. I came with the trunk that my dad had used in Officers Training School (OTS), Madras. One of its carrying handles had come off, and he had looped a rope made of cable JWD to function as a carrying handle. He has been residing in the blue sky above for the last 22 years, but as I write, the black box that carried both of us into the Army still lies right under my bed.

Good father, you did not pass gentle into that good night.
Rage, rage, rage at the dying of the light.

NDA was kinder. In OTS, on the day he reported in 1969, he had to carry this trunk on his head right to his barracks. Good old black tin trunk, you will outlast me, and the story will not find any heirs to carry you into the Army.

They billeted me in Foxtrot Squadron to spend the night. There were strict curfew orders. Nobody was supposed to switch on the light after the lights went out. The few appointments that reported early were instilling us into the ways. The wolf swarm of the real academy would descend like a tsunami after about a week.

I opened my white bed sheet and lay it on the mattress in a ground floor cabin in Foxtrot Squadron. The dinner had been strange. I had never eaten *lobiya* dal and a slice of untoasted

---

1. (Slang) In the Army, *taant* refers to a person belonging to the state of Maharashtra.

double roti with knife and fork, sitting with a stiff back. The *lobiya* tasted bland; I had never eaten it before. Who eats bread for dinner? Thank heavens, there was a little white china jug of sweet milk, which I gulped down. The chap next to me was a South Indian.

'*Me doodh nahi peetee,*' (I don't drink milk) he replied when I asked him why he was not drinking the milk. I asked if he wasn't drinking his milk, could I have it? I drank his jug, too. The waiter, the silent kind chap, got me one more jar of milk. So, well-fed on milk, I came to Foxtrot to sleep it off. Finally, I was in NDA. My eyes had roved all around—beautiful grey stone barracks that housed our Squadrons and glorious terracotta sloping roofs of each Squadron citadel. I wore the compulsory night suit as prescribed for *ikkis*[2] and sprawled out, far away from the kind warmth of a fawning mother, my favourite possessions stuffed in a large trunk at home.

I had dozed off for 10 minutes when I felt a strange itch on my butt. It felt as if a mosquito had bitten me. The bloody rules forbade switching on the lights. I scratched my burning flesh and closed my eyes. Again, something bit me on my calf. I sat up, cursed and scratched, then fell over again and slept. After a few minutes, something bit me viciously on my neck. There weren't any mosquitoes, for sure. There was no accompanying drone that forewarned of a mosquito bite. I thought, 'To hell with the rules.' I took out my steel Jeep torch and examined my lines of rashes. Then, I spied a little black bug scampering on the white sheet—a black circular thing. I had never seen a bedbug before in my life. I again lay down and tried to sleep. Before long, I was twisting and scratching all over like a madman. I got up, went out of my cabin and lay on the floor

2. (Slang) A term used to refer to the freshers or first term graduates of NDA.

of the corridor. I lay on the bare floor, scratching away at the one hundred blisters. I don't know when I fell asleep. In the morning, an orderly shook me up before PT time. He came inside and saw the blood-blotted bedsheet. He told me to wash my bed in boiling water under the bathroom geyser shower. The bed had nests of bedbugs—whole colonies in full fruition, ready for invasion.

This was a portent of gathering storms of the future. On the second day, I remember some officer interviewing me. He looked at my almost a-foot-long hair and said, 'Besides keeping hippie hair, what do you like doing?'

I replied, 'Sir, I like running.'

He kept the pen down and looked up from the form he was filling. He started laughing, 'Well, my boy, you have come to just the right place. No place like NDA for those who like running. In fact, we exist to ensure that all of you start loving running. You are allotted the Bravo Squadron.'

I thanked the Gods. I had no wish of being blood sucked by the bedbugs of the Foxtrot Squadron. I had presumed that Bravo would be free of bedbugs.

Oh, the innocence of youth!

O Rook Jaa Cadetchh!

~

Life is not what one lived, but what one remembers and how one remembers it in order to recount it.

—Gabriel Garcia Marquez

'Do you remember that time when the drill sahab, Subedar Gurmel Singh, chased you and Baidwan to the Social Science block?' Jaydee asked me on the phone.

We are from the same class of NDA, the non-technicals of '88 Batch, Section two—eight-eight two.

The Social Science block was a huge, later-addition classroom building to accommodate the wood-carving and graffiti-making non-techies, the Arts and Commerce students, simply stated, the lower orders of NDA—the 'Untermenschen'. Most of the boys, like me, were conscientious objectors to any further education. We had joined NDA to escape the torture and indecency of spending our youth enslaved to studies. We chose History and Geography to sleep through graduation, the subjects that required no mental gymnastics. Only a breed of ex-NDAs know how pleasant it can be to sleep when your cheek rests on the hard plank of your graffiti-smeared desk. On my first term break, I had asked my mother to make me a tiny pillow. She wanted to know why I wanted a six by six inch pillow. I told her that I wanted to gift it to an orphanage in Pune. She was supportive; she thought NDA was really making me a pious, piety-seeking boy. She said, '*Beta*, I will make you two. Why just one?'

I said, 'Mother, just one will be sufficient.'

When the term break ended, we boarded the NDA Special Military Train from New Delhi. When the train reached Itarsi Junction, a senior who had been making us do front rolls and push-ups most of the journey singled me out and said, 'You Fkar, here is 10 rupees. Go fly to the station. As you exit, there will be a wine shop called *Dey Daroo.* Get me a *pauwwa* of Old Monk. Vanish!'

Obedient to the unwritten laws of the Academy, I jumped across railway lines, heading straight for platform number one. I shot out of the station and found the liquor shop named *Dey Daroo.* The vendor wrapped the *pauwwa* in a newspaper, and I stuffed it in my pocket and raced back. When I had vaulted across railway tracks, I found a white hackeled drill *ustad* waiting for me. He saw the bulge in my pocket and took out the *pauwwa*, '*Accha, second term mein hi daroo peena shuru.*' (Oh, so drinking has begun in the second term itself.)

The second term started with a bang and 14 restrictions. The charge read, 'Found in possession of unauthorised drinking material and without permission leaving NDA Special.'

The pleasure of running five kilometres in hobnailed boots with full packs under the two o'clock sun was all mine. The sun-baked road with curves, bends, and slopes through forest and scrub; the clatter and thunk of boot nails; the rattle of water bottle caps and mess tins; the satisfaction of completing the restrictions till more came tumbling in your lap.

Doctor Dey was a kind professor. He taught us History and possessed a WWII Sherman tank-khaki-coloured helmet that he wore as he drove his Lambretta scooter. The helmet had circular ventilation holes all over it. It was his life's mission to teach us the Panchsheel Agreement threadbare. He took out an ancient diary, probably his own college notes from the 1950s, in which he had many large sheets folded. The sheets were all brown due to age and torn at the fold lines. He used to wear thick soda bottle glasses, and as soon as he put on his glasses and opened his Nehru-era notes, I used to take out my small pillow from my satchel, put it on my desk, rest my cheek on it, and doze off. Jaydee used to sit with me on the adjacent chair. Sometimes, Doctor Dey would enquire, 'Is that Ahlawat sleeping?'

Jaydee would say, 'No, Sir. He is studying.'

Doctor Dey was a kind soul. Some days, we all used to say, 'Sir, we are in no mood to study.'

'Okay, okay, heads down,' and the dear old man would go and stand at the classroom door to watch. If he saw any other high official coming down the corridor, he would cough discreetly and start teaching us. When the danger had passed, he would fling the chalk down and again go and stand at the door.

It's impossible to cultivate a hobby in NDA, with the perpetual boot of authority ready to smack your bum at all hours. However, I had found, like many others before me, that one got some perverse joy in adding one's own graffiti to the desks. The 50-naya-paisa ball pen refills that we carried in our pocket were our tools, along with the compass and divider of the geometry box. Nobody owned a pen all through those three years in Elysium. Michelangelo would have derived lesser divine satisfaction painting the Sistine Chapel than I did, painting my NDA classroom desks with profiles of the short and devastatingly seductive Lisa Ray and the petite, narrow-waisted, dazzling Manisha Koirala. I would often carry a page torn out of the library filmy magazines, open it on my desk, and get going with the blue refill. At least, I was doing something better than just writing, 'Screw sergeant so and so' or 'SCC so and so is a bastard'.

Jaydee was huffing a bit as he spoke, I could hear it on my mobile.

The first time I saw him, he was standing in front of the cadet's mess foyer at NDA. If I close my eyes, I still recall that picture of him in a white shirt and black trousers, his turban much tilted to one side.

'You on the treadmill, bro?' I asked.

'Yes, I was reading Maddy's articles about his time in the Army. He has named the Operation Vijay period as "Musharaff Is Dead". I asked him why not write about our class of '88, Two.' Jaydee confided.

That time was about 30 summers ago, and quite a few of us had already done our service in the Army and picked up different jobs in the civvy street.

Jaydee had also left the Army and picked up a job. It was the impersonal nature of postings all over the wilderness of our vast country that got everybody's goat. Every second year, you are on the move, uprooted, and expected to take root in an alien place with new people. Your kids, old parents, family, your kids' future, their education, admissions, everything balanced on the sharp needle point of the uncertainty of two-year postings spent out of boxes, guest rooms, fields, temporary accommodation, etc. It ended up exhausting most people, and many of my friends in my NDA graduation class were now working outside.

The last time Jaydee had called me, he had been flying currency note crates into Chhattisgarh in his helicopter for the government.

Jaydee is two metres tall, and maybe that's the reason he was able to see Gurmel chase all the way from the first battalion, across the Ashoka Circle, past the Sudan Block, and into the Mona Block so many summers ago.

One day after breakfast, I was late.

One is always tottering on the verge of the boiling oil cauldron of restrictions, Sinhagads,[3] and extra drills in NDA. Well, some chaps had mastered the ghostly art of conformity and inconspicuous passage; they never had to part with an I-slip. They went through NDA like untainted virgins who wear a salwar kameez and dupatta and walk the straight road looking down and never looking anybody in the eye. Some get mauled and ravished—more than is good for them.

That day, the wolf pack of the sergeants had left the posts after breakfast break and marched with swinging canes to their classes. The sergeants got the right to carry a cane in the fifth term, and like a new pandit who has learnt his mantras, or like a new mullah who has newly learnt his verses of the holy book, or the new pastor who has just discovered the immense power of Christ's words, they were all keen to catch some hapless worm on the wrong side of the rule book.

I was waiting in cabin number 10 on the ground floor of the Bravo Squadron, looking at the white dial of my HMT Pratap watch. I looked at the lace knots of my Oxford pattern shoes and leaned down to tighten them, and also checked the maroon garter flashes knot. The damned hassles of military dresses –

3. Sinhagad Fort overlooks NDA Khadakwasla. It is on a high promontory of the Sahiyyadri hills. A famous fort in which Shivaji's General, Tanaji Malusure, used monitor lizards carrying ropes tied to them to scale the cliff face. The Marathas captured the fort from Mughals. But Tanaji Malusure died in this attack. Shivaji famosly said, 'The fort is won but the lion is no more.' Hence, the name Sinhagad. NDA cadets are sent to touch the gates of the fort, running in battle packs, and run back to NDA. It's a 20 km run. This was the punishment meted out for minor infractions.

tassels, badges, name plates, lanyards – were all pinned into your shirt, and if any damned trinket fell off, you'd have to go into the clinker and earn a punishment.

A final look at my school days' HMT wristwatch, and I was off like a hare, one hand pressing the yellow satchel slung across. I was out of the battalion quadrangle gate when I saw another khaki-clad figure leap out like a shadow from the Alpha Squadron. Apparently, in this world, under similar circumstances, two people can decide to do the same thing. He was my classmate, Baidwan. He was also late. We both decided to make a run to the class. The stretch from the first battalion to the Social Science block, after breakfast break, is like crossing the Atlantic Ocean with lurking U-boats. We decided to make a run through Operation Paukenschlag. Chances of running into a prowling U-boat in the form of an officer, drill sahab, sergeant, appointments, etc., and being torpedoed and sunk were very high. We set our course towards Ashoka and ran steadily at a canter. As far as our eyes could see, there were no sergeants lurking on the Trishul Marg, and we thought we were lucky to have a clear run. In the far distance, the last of the squads was marching up the Sudan slope. We were two squadless interlopers, ordinary cadets running independently—a crime of the first water in the laws of NDA—an unimpeachable sacrilege in the scheme of things of NDA.

Both of us were almost congratulating ourselves on making the Great Escape look like child's play. We had not bothered to cover our tail, content with straight-nosed sprinting only. A loud roar broke the stillness and sound of our padding feet, '*O rook jaa cadetecch!'* (Stop, cadet!)

Baidwan was a Sikh. I told him not to turn back. I was a beret-clad ordinary cadet of medium height. Hundreds of them are of my make and model. I turned my neck and saw the bicycle mounted by Gurmel Singh pedalling as fast as he could towards us like the battleship *Bismarck* cutting through the Scapa Flow.

'Who is it?' asked Baidy.

'Gurmel Singh sahab of Sikh Light Infantry,' I replied.

Gurmel Singh sahab was one of my favourite drill sahabs. He looked very funny, and I had always wanted to sketch him with blue refills on the classroom desks. He was a man with an enormous belly and, in the scheme of things, not the most agile of men. And here he was, trying to catch up with two very athletic 18-year-olds and hollering, *'O rook jaa cadetchh!'*

Had we stopped, he would have taken our I-slips, and the Squadron flashboard would have carried our names to come to Adjutant's *durbar* on the steps of the Sudan Block—a very painful affair because of the dress requirement. Your dress had to be perfect, new, and freshly starched. The starched KDs were a pain-in-the-ass kind of clothes. Depending on the Adjutant's mood, you could come from the *durbar* with a harvest of punishments for things like boots not shining, insignias not brassed, shabby dress, shave not proper, haircut not done, improper salute, not standing at proper attention, giving meaningful looks, etc. All in addition to the original offence for which your I-slip had been taken. You had to avoid getting caught at all costs for the sake of sheer survival.

Gurmel was chugging with the boilers at full horsepower and gaining on us. We saw a foot track through the grass leading towards the NDA telephone exchange. Leaving the beaten track, i.e., leaving the roads, was another goddamned offence in that land of petty offences, capable of destroying your military career before it had even sprouted. Both of us left the road, dived into the grass, and started climbing uphill towards the Mona Block. The Social Science block had earned the moniker due to the presence of a very pretty teacher there.

We saw the turbaned Gurmel Singh turn his bicycle to climb up the Sudan slope. He was putting all his strength on the pedals, and for the poor chap, it was so much of an effort, for he was a portly senior Subedar on the verge of retirement. He let out yet another breathless and plaintive cry, *'O rook jaa cadetchh!'*

I have wondered why most of them had their own ways of pronouncing cadet. The last squad marching up the Sudan had our classmate Jaydee, the tall one, in it. He had been seeing the whole thing from his majestic seven-foot lighthouse height. 'I had thought you guys would slip away into the Mona Block unmolested,' he told us later on.

When we were on the verge of victory, we decided to do something inexplicable. We stood on the road and waited for Gurmel Singh sahab to catch up with us.

He had to get off his bicycle and walk or run it up the Sudan slope. Now he pedalled towards us, his face and beard all soaked in perspiration. Baidwan, being a Sardar, spoke to him in Punjabi, 'Sahab, you know we could have escaped. There is no chance you could have caught us.'

Gurmel Singh looked at us steadily, his pen poised on his notepad, ready to register our offence and particulars. He was still breathing very hard, his round torso rising and falling.

'We stopped because we thought you might have a heart attack if we made you exert more. Now, you decide whether you want to put us up or not for punishment,' Baidwan continued.

That was pretty audacious of Baidwan, and in the end, he won. Gurmel shut his notebook and told us not to get late for classes in future and turned away his bicycle.

Jaydee was saying that we must write about our NDA days and our NDA class. Baidy is now a US citizen, and Jaydee flies civil choppers. He just off-handedly said, 'You two chaps, running away from the drill sahab, went on to earn gallantry awards later on in your careers. Baidy got a Shaurya Chakra, and you got a Sena Medal Gallantry. And I heartily laugh whenever I think of that moment: two decorated soldiers running away like hounds, and Gurmel sahab pedalling nineteen to the dozen on your tail shouting, *"O rook jaa cadetchh, o rook jaa cadetchh!"*" I wanted to tell Jaydee that it's easier to face the enemy in battle than the wrath of an angry NDA drill sahab. Or at least, that's how it looks now after so many years.

We Came

~

I was going out into the desert with my own group of scorpions. My first independent reconnaissance.

We had two Jongas and one Jeep. Canvas water bags (*chaugals*) hung around our four-wheel drive Jongas like garlands. The Jonga was a notoriously powerful jeep that skimmed over the dunes with ease. It was the hot summer season, and only those who have lived in the Thar Desert know what real heat is.

The desert scorpions had to be on friendly terms with temperatures over 120°F. One day, we started a little party with three jeeps, aiming to explore the whole area running along the Radcliffe Line, that is, our western border. When we entered the dunes, the vehicles started overheating, and their tyres were deflated halfway. They ran well over the sand, but the heat was all-conquering. Where was the water to pour over scalding radiators? I realised the futility of being out during the day. So, we started avoiding moving about in the hottest hours of the day.

There is a desert plant that grows a lot around Jaisalmer. It's called *bhui*. *Bhui* is quite a wonder plant; it looks like congress grass with snowflake-like flowers that bloom in the winter season. We sucked on *bhui* roots, and it did help slake the thirst. If you cut a lot of it and throw it in a sand pit, it also works as good bedding.

So, we progressed every day, marking our routes on the maps and relying on the prismatic compass to get our bearings. Navigation in the desert is an engrossing study that lacks defined landmarks. Stars are very helpful guides to those who can read them.

As our reconnaissance progressed, we crossed Baap La Talao. Then, we came across a mud-brick fort in the middle of nowhere called *Bacchia Chor Ka Quila* (Bacchia Thief's Fort). This was a cattle smuggler's fort where livestock was exchanged for opium and other commodities in the frontier-less free trade of bygone years.

We kept going westwards, hoping to spot a border pillar, but there was no sign of one. We saw a *mazaar* (grave) at a distance and drove there. It was a simple grave exposed to the sun, wind, and sand. A green *chadar* (cloth) with a filigree border lay over the grave, held in place by stones kept over its borders. We decided to take a break there. Somebody took out the stove and brewed tea quickly. I looked around as I sipped my tea, and my eyes fell on the currency notes and coins that lay about the *mazaar*. I bent down and picked up a ten-rupee note and kept staring at it. My second-in-command, Subedar Bairam Khan, saw my expression and came to enquire. His eyes nearly popped out of their sockets when they fell upon the karakul-capped picture of Quaid-e-Azam, Muhammad Ali Jinnah, on the currency note.

'*Sahab, hum to Pakistan ke andar ghussey huey hain.*' (Sir, we are well inside Pakistan.)

I nodded and did a 360-degree sweep of the horizons. For the time being, there were no speeding jeeps coming to capture us. I walked to the bonnet of the Jonga and took out a fountain pen from my breast pocket.

I wrote on the Pakistani currency note.

WE CAME
1. Captain Angrez Singh

Then, Subedar Bairam Khan wrote his name under mine in his own hand, followed by every member of our troop. When all the autographs were done, I drew a scorpion on the note and left it on the *mazaar*, with a little stone over it as a paperweight.

In a few more days, we completed all the tasks that had been set out for us. Everybody was sworn to silence by the *omertà* code of comrades. The incident of the stray gallop inside Pakistan and back never happened. It was buried and salted; all mouths tamped shut. It felt nice being back in the unit, taking a bath, and scrubbing off the two week's layers of salt, sweat, and dirt that had formed black half-moons under the nails. Eating fresh chappatis and dal and a cool bowl of curd was such a bliss and utter joy to the senses. To sleep on a clean and nice-smelling bed after days and days of the fetid smell of unwashed bodies and sweat-caked clothes—ah, the joy!

The next day, I reported our return to the CO. He asked about the reconnaissance and our day-wise routes and distances covered and drawn on the map. Then he asked, 'All went well, I suppose?'

'Yes, Sir. Couldn't have gone better. Everything as planned.'

That's the golden operative phrase of the Army, say it, and all seniors are happy.

'Did anything unusual happen?'

'No, nothing at all, Sir.'

'Sure?'

'Sure, Sir.'

He pulled open the drawer of his desk and laid a Pakistani note on the desk. Then, he picked it up and started reading out aloud, 'We Came. Number One, Captain Angrez Singh, Number Two, Subedar Bairam Khan, etc., etc.'

I stood impassive, and my mind raced in circles. How the hell did the CO come to know? Who snitched? I quickly ran my radar over all my teammates. They were all solid chaps. It couldn't be anyone from my troop.

The CO said, 'And did you really think I will leave a young Captain on his first independent troop level recce unobserved? Dismiss.'

I came out, scratching my head. A few local leather-faced Rajasthani men in dhoti and thick leather *juttis* hung about the Subedar Major's office. And then, the riddle fell open.

Of course, the CO had his favourite desert dogs trailing us, the Khojis. They had visited the *mazaar* after us and brought back the incriminating currency note that the CO had in his drawer.

The Crossover Girl

~

The girl was walking across the minefield. She had the light-footed walk of a girl born and bred in the hills. It looked as if she was not aware of the little explosive devices mixed in the old soil that could take off those dove-like legs of hers. The red fleck of her garment nodded like a solitary rose through the wild grass that grew in the minefield. Rarely did anyone take such a fool's walk.

The bored Sepoy at the Kali Billey post had been on duty in his bunker during the after-breakfast shift. He kept aside his mobile phone and rubbed his eyes in a quick circular movement. He again ran his eyes across the minefield that merged into the mist-covered border called the Line of Control (LoC). There was no sign of anything. He thought that he had seen an apparition, something red-coloured in the grass. He watched a little longer and then returned to watching the movie on his mobile phone. The white letters 'AV' embroidered on the left shoulder of his battle dress denoted his rank. He was an Agniveer, a new rank of a new India and new commercial times. Nothing happened on the LoC; the Kali Billey post was an oasis of peace. His rifle lay on the embrasure wall. A steel chain secured the rifle to his belt like a dog on duty.

Every now and then, the boy soldier would pause his movie and look up with his rodent-like cunning eyes. He would cock his ear to catch sounds from the direction of the narrow footpath that served his post. He would hear the unvarying sounds of boredom made by the jungle, then peer out towards the LoC and again return to kill the time of his watch. He checked the battery on his mobile phone. It was almost three-fourths consumed. He patted the box pocket of his combat jacket and felt the heavy mass of the power bank. He had told his fellow soldier to get another fully charged power bank when he returned from the company headquarters in the evening.

He gloated when he saw the hero in the movie ride a Yamaha speed bike; the girl sitting behind him had hardly any perch space. She hugged the taut back of the hero like a magnet on the refrigerator. This scene thrilled the boy soldier, and he thought that he would demand this very model of bike in *dahez* (dowry). Then, a doubt passed his crew-cut head. He was an AV. How much could he demand in the marriage deal? He pushed the unpleasant thought aside. He would break into guffaws of laughter when the comedian of the flick made sour and vulgar *bhabhi* jokes. And again, his animal watchfulness would start listening to sounds. He was scared of the young Captain who was the Company Commander. Although not much older than himself, the Company Commander was a martinet and had prohibited using mobile phones while on sentry duty. If he got caught, his little world would become very tense and his existence very tiring. He reminded himself that he shouldn't get caught at any cost. His back was stiff from watching the mobile screen too much. He got up to stretch himself and decided to walk about a bit.

The LoC was serene, sterile, and green, like the Lodhi Gardens of Delhi. The post dog wagged his tail two times and closed his lazy eyes again. It was a seasoned dog that had found that the boundaries of life ran from one *langar* or post to the next. He was sleeping because it was a heavy effort to digest oil hydro pooris that he had had for breakfast along with the *jawans*. The soldier walked out whistling and stood with his back to the LoC. He was observing the foot track that connected his post to the rear. His eyes scanned the entire stretch yard by yard, and only then was he satisfied that all was well.

He took out his mobile and thought of making a video for Instagram. However, it was forbidden to make videos of posts. He satisfied himself by taking a few selfies and then checking the pictures in the phone gallery. His complexion seemed to be sunburnt. He made a mental note to buy some Fair and Lovely fairness cream for himself the next time he went to the canteen. He put his phone in his pocket and again started loitering. Sometime later, he took out his mobile phone and looked at the time. There was still one hour to lunch when his buddies would come carrying the steel tiffins full of dal, roti, *sabzi*, and *chawal*.

When he raised his head to look towards the LoC, he saw a figure emerge from a growth of wild bushes. A girl dressed in a red *phiran* was walking towards his post. He thought it most unusual. Nobody came there, least of all a female. He shook his head as if he was shaking off honey bees and then gazed in her direction again; she was coming straight towards his post. He looked at the seasoned dog. Its mouth lay open, and its pink tongue lay like a bubble gum between its teeth. The sun warmed its black and white fur as it kept sleeping. He called out to the dog, hoping that it would bark a warning and make the woman go away, whoever she was. The dog ignored his slights and kept sleeping with great dignity. It was the old dog of the post, grown up there since it was a pup, and had fought off many an invader for 10 years. It would be damned if it would react to this young pipsqueak of an AV. The dog acted only when prodded, at the minimum by a Junior Commissioned Officer (JCO). The creature was aware of his privileges.

When the female form closed in, the AV saw that she was not a grown-up woman but a young girl not yet out of teenage. The newness of her nose and eyes, the slim neck, and the quickness of her limbs as she walked were apparent. She had a scarf tied on her head. She had seen him standing from a distance and was coming straight at him. He kept standing and followed her progress. She came and stood beneath the bunker and said, '*Pani pilao*.' (Give me some water to drink.)

He had been watching her in a rapture of strange fear and delight. A part of him instinctively understood that she would only mean *lafdaa* or trouble. But when he saw her, her beauty and newness gladdened a sense inside him that welcomed the exquisite creations of earth. He walked quickly inside and got a two-litre Pepsi bottle filled with water and a Borosil glass. Then, he filled the glass with clean, cool water and gave it to the girl. She had wiry, strong hands with the nails of a working girl. Blue veins stood out startlingly bold on her thin ivory skin. She drank the water quickly and extended her hand for more. She drank again. The old dog of the post, who had been sleeping, opened his eyes and shook his ears. The soldier looked at the girl's jaw and neck as she drank—how the supple neck moved in ripples with the water!

The girl wiped her mouth with her sleeves, and he saw that her clothes were full of wattles and thorn bulbs that had stuck to her clothes as she walked across Ultima Thule. He looked at her more and realised that she was just like girls on this side of the LoC. Their constitution was small, narrow, and extremely slim. He had thought that it must have something to do with their staple food of mountain corn, that they called *dodaa*. The girl wore canvas and rubber-soled shoes that were worn by the school and college-going girls of this side of the LoC. He started feeling like a fool. His mind felt vacant and irresolute. He felt shy and tongue-tied in her presence.

'Would you like to eat something if you are hungry?' he croaked. It had taken effort, an overcoming of insolvent shyness that is tougher than running a five-kilometre beepty run. He felt victorious over his mind. He marvelled secretly at his on-the-spot inventiveness. Only a few moments ago, he had felt the panic in his mind. He had felt that the thinking frog that sat in his mind had left his cranium.

The girl said nothing, and he turned and walked inside the post. He found an unopened one-litre tetra pack of milk, and a tin of Amul Milkmaid (condensed milk). He picked up both of them and came out of the dark bunker post. The girl was still sitting on the large stone just as he had left her. He walked up to her in an inhibited manner and said, 'There are only these two things, nothing else.' He thought with wistfulness that it would have been so much better if he had kept two oil hydro pooris to give the girl. But the fat old veteran dog had the first claim to the surplus breakfast pooris. The girl took both the articles and tried to read what was written on them. She opened her thin, delicate lips and read the bold print.

'Amm...ool. A mullah. Amm tool,' she tried to pronounce the strange words in various sounds.

'What does it say, and what does it contain?' she spoke in a heavy, hill-accented Hindustani, but the soldier understood her.

'It's Amul condensed milk, very sweet and tasteful. But we have been using it for so long that it has lost its flavour. Now it's just another boring food stuff.'

'Amul. What a name! What does it mean?' she asked.

'I don't know. It isn't a word from my part of the country,' replied the soldier.

'Which is your part of the country?' prodded the girl.

'Haryana. My village is near Rohtak,' came the reply.

The girl kept the tin on the ground and said, 'You come from the region of the wrestler girls. The girls who win India medals in sports.'

'Yes,' nodded the young soldier.

'I have a teacher in our college. She once said, "Women are equal to men in every way. Look at these Indian sisters of yours. They win medals in such sports like wrestling and boxing." Do you know any of them? Babita, Ritu, and the others?'

'No, I don't,' the soldier said. He opened the tetra pack, filled the glass with milk, and extended his hand to the girl, 'Have it. It's the only thing I can offer you.'

The girl took the glass and started laughing, 'What's your name?'

'Sultan Singh,' he said.

The girl said, 'Sultan Bhai, I haven't come all the way from Pakistan to drink this imitation milk.'

The boy soldier was confused about her motives, 'What's your name, sister?'

'Nigar Kausar,' replied the girl.

'Then, what have you come here for? Don't you know this is India, and you just can't walk across and come here?' he asked. He had started feeling the tightness of apprehension in his chest—the apprehension of rules, drills, and SOPs they kept ranting about in durbars, fall-ins, and *sainik sammelans*. There were mountain ranges of rules and instructions—smouldering slag heaps of rules for everything under the sky, as big as Ghazipur *murga mandi* (chicken market).

'I have two legs, and Allah has given me life to explore. I am a free person,' she said.

'I go wherever my fancy takes me. Allah has himself commanded that the faithful must go in search of new knowledge. It's written in the holy book,' continued the girl.

Sultan heard the girl attentively. Then, he said, 'I am sure Allah doesn't tell you to take foolish risks. You know you walked right through a minefield. Had you stepped on a mine, you would have been conversing with your Allah's fairies!'

She seemed perplexed. She asked him what a mine was. He explained to her by digging a hole in the ground and keeping an empty tin in it. He covered it with mud. Just a tiny bit of the lid showed. Then, he stepped on the tin and shouted, 'Baddaamm!' and fell down, clutching his leg in agony.

Nigar watched the sunburnt Indian, who just had a thin line of moustache sprouting on his upper lip, with joy and fascination. Then she said, 'Everything happens by Allah's command. I live because He commands it.'

Sultan found her nonchalance unique. Yet, he doubted the strength of her common sense. He had forgotten to ask her the most important question. Now that he felt that the initial ice wall of shyness inside him had started melting, he asked her, 'Sister, why have you come to India?'

The girl started tittering and laughing, 'You will think me a real *ahmak* (fool), but anyhow, I must tell you.'

She opened the hand-embroidered cloth purse that she was carrying and took out a page. She had written on it in Urdu script. She unfolded it to reveal a lined page of an ordinary notebook that students use.

'This is a list of Hindi movies I have come to watch. All Shah Rukh Khan movies. I have saved some money. I will be spending my own money.'

Sultan's mouth fell open. The girl was suicidally brave, enchanted, and daft. The Gods had unnecessarily given so much beauty to a silly, bull-headed girl like her.

'You have come to watch Hindi movies? You have come to watch films!' he kept repeating his words, trying to digest the girl's motives, and shook his head in disbelief. Human beings are differently driven and in love with unforeseen passions. This girl was either too innocent or plain splendidly mad.

'Don't you have cinema in Pakistan?' he asked.

'We have, but I know that in India, nobody prohibits women and girls from watching cinema all alone. On my side, I can't ever go to a cinema hall all alone. Only the men go to watch movies,' she told the soldier.

He looked at her calmly. What stepmotherly hell she lived in, he thought. His own sister went to college all alone every day. Girls were becoming independent and ruthlessly feminist even in his village at a fast pace. They were crushing the old chains in a flood of liberation. The tiger of suppression was old now. It was time to hack it into small pieces and kick it into the dirt. They were refusing to get married when forced into bad marriages. There was a tide of social improvement in India. There were fiercely independent female Members of Parliament, and the President of the country was a lady. He thought about how easily we took our liberties and how cheaply we regarded such freedoms. India was a paradise that had exercised its sway on Nigar.

Nigar got up to go, 'Show me the way to Naushera. I have relatives living there. I will live with them and go to watch movies on my own.'

She shook her purse and coins jingled inside, 'I have saved enough money.'

He looked her doubtfully in the face, 'Beyond here, you will run into more and more Army. They are bound to question you about where you have come from. Do you have an identity card issued by the district administration or an Indian Aadhar Card?'

The girl tightened her lips and stretched them wide in a gesture of despair.

'Then I will suggest, sister, you go back the way you came,' advised the youngling.

The girl stared at him. Her eyes had bold disagreement in them, 'I didn't come all the way to go back without watching the movies.'

He thought about his own position. It was she who had been the red fleck he had seen in the distance, and he had casually been watching movies on his mobile. What was he supposed to do? Shoot her? He was just an Agniveer. He had a few more months to go since the Army would kick him out high and dry. To hell with it, he thought. He would not taint his hands with any *paap* on his life's *patri.* The girl was the age of his sister. He wondered whether his own sister was capable of doing such a mad and audacious caper. He had himself given the minefield wires a wide margin by far. Who was interested in taking unnecessary *pangaas* being an Agniveer? If he died, his family would not get a pie or a *footi-cowdie* in pension. Foolish girl, he thought, utterly foolhardy. He looked at her again and thought, God has made her so beautiful, yet this daft girl walks through this minefield to watch movies. What should be his next action? He didn't bother much if they threw him out. As it is, they would do it after one year. Who cares?

He decided to tell her clearly how the matter stood, 'Nigar, you will have to go back taking the exact same foot marks that you took. If they catch you, they will put you in jail or something. I don't know what will become of you. Seriously, I am not bothered about myself. For me, what's there to be bothered about? I am like a contractual hired security guard working here for *rozi-roti.* It's about you that I am bothered. Please go back home.'

The girl was obdurate. She was in love with India and Indian films. She had come with faith and hope. God knows what a hate-free and ignorant family she had been brought up in that she had no prejudices, fears, or dangers etched in her mind. Her worldview was not right. She should have been seething and dripping with putrid fear, hatred, religiosity, and venom. As if he cared a damn! He was just an AV on contract. He decided to pass the buck. It is dangerous for a poor man to think of honour, valour, and sacrifice on an empty stomach. He walked inside the bunker and rotated the crank of the field telephone set. After ten minutes of furious rotations, a man picked up the phone and barked, *'Abey kya hai Kali Billey?'* (What the hell is it, Kali Billey post?)

He steadied his voice, 'Sir, I want to inform the senior JCO *sahab* that we have a visitor from across at the Kali Billey post.'

'Has a dog crossed over and come?' asked the bored man at the other end of the line.

'Nahi, Sir. Ek ladki.' (No, Sir. A girl.)

The senior JCO *sahab* was having chai and wasn't reachable on the phone. The telephone operator, who was not a man to dam up the flow of information, flicked the Company Commander's phone switch.

'*Haan, bol,*' (Yes, speak) answered the annoyed Company Commander. The Captain was studying for IAS Mains entrance exams and disliked interruptions. His orders to the exchange were that only the CO should be patched up to him, and only in an extreme emergency, 'Disturb me only if a nuclear bomb is falling. For all other purposes, I am out on patrol or ambush. Understood?'

'Sahab, Kali Billey post on line,' said the operator quickly and linked the connection. On the other end, passing the buck back to Captian Sahab, Agniveer Sultan asked, 'Ram-ram, Sahab. A girl has come here. What should I do?' Captain IAS was in no mood to get entangled in frivolous matters. He had to get back to his books. He said to AV Sultan Singh, 'Tell her to return to wherever she came from.' He had no interest in these useless matters. He was an ex-NDA Agniveer Max Pro entry into the Army. He knew the chances were high that many like him would get the aluminium handshake and not make it to the permanent cadre-authorised pensions. Who knew what would happen in the future? The *sarkar* was playing Russian Roulette and changed rules every day, making senior officers announce them in press conferences. The government, it seemed, had gone highly wise and profit-oriented. And when the world was being given bananas, the best thing was to pass the banana. He thought that he would pass the banana and get back to his books. He got a call through to his CO and promptly gave the banana to his Colonel, 'Sir, a girl has come to the Kali Billey post. Duly reporting, over and out. Line bad, Sir. Can't talk any further.'

The Colonel, who was drinking Knorr tomato soup in his office, missed a few heartbeats. Then, he calmed himself and took a small pill out of his medicine box. His blood pressure was unduly high, as it is. Such sudden bloopers would give him a heart attack someday, he thought. He had not reported his blood pressure problem to Army doctors. He was an aspiring Colonel who was receiving treatment at Gupta Hospital in Punjabi Bagh. He had found an acupuncturist in Najafgarh who poked pins and got his blood pressure to normal just prior to the annual medical examination. He thought that a 'blood pressure low' medical category would finish all his ambitions of becoming Army Commander. However, the way things were going, he felt the flame of ambition sputtering like an oil lamp that finds water mixed in the kerosene. He felt his heart jump like a frog in a well. He took a deep breath and did what he was good at—passing the banana to his Commander.

The Commander sahab still had some rudiments of old

Army intact inside his frame. When told that a girl had jay-walked inside from across, he went to the battalion to investigate. When he reached there, he found that Nigar was still at the Kali Billey post. The needle of initiative had stopped like a Quartz clock that runs out of battery.

Brigadier Zilley Singh walked to Kali Billey. He knew this was his zenith rank. He had failed to sell himself upwards. But he had not lost his old habit of walking to the bull and catching it by the horns. The Brigadier was a product of pre-Agniveer times. He did not understand this era of hidden contractual clauses, small prints, and empty pockets at the end of it.

In the meantime, at the Kali Billey post, the langar tiffin had arrived. Sultan and his buddy Multan Singh were laying out the *dongaas* on a field table. Nigar was picking off thorns from her shawl and salwar and had taken off her shoes. Brigadier Zilley Singh arrived at the post. The post dog had gotten up and sat next to Nigar, who was petting his grizzled old head. He raised his eyes to look at the new arrival. The old dog noted the star-crowded shoulder epaulettes of the Brigadier sahab and gave his old tail two extra rotations of welcome to the senior officer.

Sultan saw the perspiring face of Brigadier Zilley Singh rise up from the rim of the path. The Brigadier visited the post at least once a month to make sure that the LoC had not tectonically shifted eastwards while his mobile-addicted Agniveers were watching Sapna Choudhary's pelvic gyrations and bosom-ic upheavals.

Zilley noted that his physical fitness had gone down despite the steady diet of two desi ghee parathas he had every morning after his two-kilometre jog, 50 push-ups, and 50 sit-ups. He had tried to do his duty correctly all his life. Sycophancy had failed to make dents into his soldierly fabric. Any senior official visiting his domain was told that he was expected to pay the proper mess bill—no complimentary single malts or gift hampers here. He paid for whatever he consumed, the same as the junior officers. He was the sort of officer who paid for his own newspaper and electricity bill and did not get the bathrooms Jaquar-ised from the Military Engineering Services (MES).

Sultan, who saw the Commander Sahab, came to attention and called out a loud, 'Ram-ram, Sahab.' He put all his Agniveer energy into a curdling yell that made Nigar's heart skip a beat in fear. What meteor was falling on their heads, she thought, that they scream as if a dagger pierceth their hearts.

Zilley could see the girl petting the jowly post dog. She was a beautiful, tough, wild rose of a being. Zilley was that unusual relic of a man of an earlier mould who derived his joy from dipping into poetry and bird watching rather than getting the tiles of his house changed from MES before moving in. He had read *The Aeneid* a couple of times. Virgil's words rang in his head:

Don't trust the horse Trojans
Whatever it is,
I fear the Greeks even bearing gifts.

This girl, this charming Trojani horse from across the LoC, was like the Greek Sea that separated Troy. He was deeply mistrustful of the 'Pak**tani' Greeks, and his wisdom from the ancient poets was chiming a warning—*beware! This could be a trap.* He followed the senior officers' habit of carrying toffees and chocolates in his pocket to do walking *sadbhavna.* He felt inside his satchel and fished out a canteen store's bar of 5Star chocolate.

Nigar, who was observing him, felt that this new arrival must be the big officer around here. She slid her shoes onto her feet and got up. She smiled, and did an Indian sort of *namaste* to Zilley. He walked to the girl and gave her the 5Star, and the girl thanked him. One of the Agniveers walked up to the Commander and said, *'Roti khaa lo saab.'* (Sir, have some food.)

The *jawans* had placed upturned ammunition boxes and a tin to serve as stools. Zilley looked at his watch and said to Nigar, 'Please have something to eat. You can eat with us or sit separately.'

The girl seemed to be having the adventure of her life amidst the kaffirs. She smiled and said that she would sit with them. Zilley gave her a steel plate and spoon. The girl hesitated.

'You are our *mehmaan* (guest). You first,' he said.

The girl helped herself to some dal, *subzi*, and roti. The old dog of the post came and sat next to her with timeless patience, smelling the aroma of turmeric and flour chappatis wafting around this simple military table.

Zilley noticed that the Agniveers Sultan and Multan had kept their mobile phones next to their plates. With half an eye, they kept a watch on the notification bar of the phone. Zilley, who was nearly half a century old, noticed the habits of the new boys. He thought that had they shown half as much attentiveness to the job at hand, this girl – like a queen of trouble – would not be sitting with them.

Nigar was saying a silent prayer for the food. The two Haryanvi clods had produced a desi ghee *dabba* and extended it to the Brigadier Sahab. The old dog was observing the roundels of flight that a flea was making around his head. Zilley picked up a chappati and dusted it on one side. He was a Sainik School boy and had retained this peculiar habit. Even in parties and dinners in formal settings, Zilley would absent-mindedly pick a chappati and dust it noisily. He tore the roti and, with the other hand, pushed the desi ghee towards the girl. She spooned out a little on her dusty chappati doubtfully. She was debating whether she should also dust the chappati in the same fashion. She thought it would appear rude and dropped the idea.

'Young lady, what brings you to kaffir country?' Zilley addressed Nigar in mild tones. Evidently, the child was either very courageous or very stupid to have loitered across the unverifiable and badly marked minefields of old wars.

'Sir, I came hoping to watch some films of my choice. I know girls have more freedom here,' she fumbled in her cloth bag, took out the notebook slip, and gave it to Zilley. Zilley looked at the lines, curves, and arcs of Urdu script and nodded his head. He had read Urdu for three terms under Mr Ansari at the NDA. Poor Mr Ansari had died long ago. God rest his soul in peace! He had made him sit on the first bench and ensured he learnt the versatile language of poets. The Brigadier had lost touch with the language and couldn't read the list. He handed her the page.

Next, he turned his attention to the busy Agniveers who were making *chapdak-chapdak* sounds as they ate in native Haryanvi fashion. Zilley pitied these boys. It was still a wonder that some of them cared to join up under the new cockeyed scheme. He was curious to learn about the troops under his command. He chewed his chappati slowly and turned to Sultan, 'Young man, what motivated you to join the Army?'

Sultan kept his roti down. He looked at Zilley and then grasped his tummy with both hands, 'This, Sir. Hunger is such a thing that it can make a person take food out of another person's mouth and eat it. One has to do some work or starve. I come from a very poor family. There is a retired *fauji* in my village who tells the young boys like me in my village:

Bharti ho jyaa rey rangroot.
Aade miley tootey leetar
Uddey millaan gey boot.

Bharti ho jyaa rey rangroot
Aadey milleyen gaali dhoppad
Uddey milleyen gey salute.

Bharti ho jyaa rey rangroot
Addey millyen sookhey teekadd
Uddey milleyen gey khaana ne biscoot

Boy enroll as a recruit (*rangroot*)
Here you wear torn slippers
There you will get proper boots.

Boy enroll as a recruit
Here you get taunts and insults
There you will get a salute.

Boy enroll as a recruit
Here you get dry old chappati
There you will get to eat biscuit.

Zilley enjoyed this crude Haryanvi doggerel. He silently applauded the bravura of Sultan. The boy seemed a frank and uninhibited chatterbox.

Zilley asked, 'What will you do after you finish your Agniveer contract?'

'Sir, I will go to Bombay or Canada. I am young; I know how to do many things. In the foreign countries, they pay well for work, and many things are assured there,' answered the soldier boy.

'But what about country, patriotism, *Bharat mata ki raksha?* Who will do that?' enquired the Commander.

'Sahab, look at it like this. India has millions of poor hungry boys like me. The recruitment lines will never break. India has no dearth of cheap cannon fodder, and the bureaucrats and politicians know it. But there is another condition under which we have come. If at the end of your Brigadiery, the *sarkar* does not give you the pension and facilities of ex-servicemen, you, yourself, Sahab, will not stick around in the Army for two days extra. That's the reality, Sahab. We know what all this Agniveer-Shagniveer business is,' the boy replied, munching on his food.

Zilley had noticed that these Agniveer boys behaved like curious visitors with an attitude of non-participation and non-interest. They behaved like friendly spectators. They felt nothing at stake. They felt they had no share in whatever was asked of them to do. They felt like shadows in this landscape. They weren't real soldiers, and the term was an insult to them. In their hearts, they had no doubt that they were the discardable Sepoys, paper napkins meant to be used and chucked.

Zilley noticed with disquiet this fraying of the sinews of the old solid system. A decline in courage was the most striking feature. Such a decline in courage was also noticeable in the leadership. The halls of leadership were teeming with Uncle Tom's. They radiated the impression of loss of courage. In contrast, and like a comedy of errors, this Faustian bargain expected courage and sacrifice from the poor pawns of the chessboard.

Nigar ate the tasteless, cold food. She pecked at the food that was not to her taste. She had that habit of going hungry if the food did not suit her taste. So far, she had not landed into any trouble in the kaffir land. It was a happy discovery to her that the kaffirs were human after all. If the ranting *mullahs* were to be believed, nothing was going well in the kaffir world. She thought that this silver-headed Brigadier, their senior officer, had no airs about himself. She wondered if she had unnecessarily put them all in a quandary by arriving as an unwelcome guest. The pull of India was too much in her blood with the inebriation of its cinema.

'Will you not be missed at your home?' asked Zilley, who had given up his reverie about the new genome strain being injected into the Army.

Nigar smiled insouciantly and said, 'My family knows I have gone to visit relatives for three days. Nobody will miss me for three days, and had I been allowed to go to the town, I would have been watching *Pathan* movie already.'

The Brigadier had underestimated the crossover girl's resourcefulness. He was speculating this fine business. Nigar stayed on in India for two days. Zilley's daughter took her in his white Alto to the theatre, and Nigar watched her favourite movies till the cinema started overflowing from her heart. Then, it was time for her to return to her country.

Zilley stood at the Kali Billey post and watched her walk back across the LoC. The old dog of the post was walking with her as if he had decided to do one noble deed in his life besides eating fauji ration and sleeping. She disappeared from view. Zilley slept at Kali Billey that night. The next morning, he trained his spotter scope on a distant village across and onto a white house with a green roof. A white bedsheet lay drying on the green roof. This was Nigar's pre-decided signal that she had reached home safe and sound. He felt there was something written on the white sheet. He increased the magnification of his spotter scope. The impish girl had written something on the sheet.

Thank you. Can I revisit?

Zilley's tenure was about to end, and he did not wish that the Trojan Horse would come again.

As Virgil had said in *The Aeneid*:

I fear the Greeks even when they bring gifts.

Theory of Military Relativity

~

There was a flamboyant Punjabi neighbour of mine who had an adage he adhered to truthfully. The adage was about rum and whisky—a thumb rule as true as Newton's laws. But this story, I hope, will prove the 'Theory of Military Relativity' as true, with due apologies to Herr Professor Einstein.

He was a smart set Armoured Corps officer who believed in the fact that the smartness of things mattered. Everything about him was smart. His car was smart; his Bullet, with a regimental crest and booming ear-shattering exhaust pipe, was smart. His children were smart, his wife was smart, and her perfume, which left a two-furlong wake, was smart. Even his *sahayak* was smart. And like all affluent and posh officers of Punjab, he, too, came from Shann-dee-garrh, the city of their heart.

Chandigarh was the brainchild of PM Nehru, the first artificial show-off city of India designed by the French architect Le Corbusier after independence. Thank God Pandit Nehru didn't call the new town Pandit Puri, Moghul Puri, Nehru Puri, Amrit Puri, Amrit Garh, Nehruabad, Hindu Nagar, or some such name sweating of religious purity. Our new Islamic cousins built their own new show-off town and called it Islamabad. I am sure Islamabad must have a lot of Islam, as an armoured regiment has a lot of tanks, and a signal regiment has a lot of telephones. I don't know whether Chandigarh has a fortress built by some medieval man called Baba Chanda Singh, but then the name should have been properly called Chandagarh or Chanda Singh Walla. Saint Google tells me that the town is named after a Chandi Mata temple.

But I digress; let's go back to my neighbour and the Theory of Military Relativity. My neighbour used to have his daily tipple sitting on his balcony. It was invariably a bottle of Old Monk rum. Sometimes, he used to call me over to have a drink with him as the sun set. I think such a drink is called a sundowner by educated 'Shandigarh' folks. He used to say:

Bahar piyo whiskey,
Kadon iss di, kadon uss di.
Garh vich piyo rum,
De danaa dan dann.

(Outside of home,
Drink other people's fine whiskey.
At home,
Make do with rum.)

It reminded me of the time when I had once been made the mess secretary of my unit's officer's mess. My CO was a very ambitious officer, and his boss, the *jarnail saab* (General), had reached the scratch handicap as far as promotions were concerned. One day, the CO called me to his office. I had immediately put in the leave application after being proposed and seconded to be the mess secretary. He was glowering over the leave application like a stray bull glowers over a trash heap that only contains polythene waste.

'I must say you have timed your leave application well. Can I say that it is not related to your being made mess secretary?' he looked up like a master looks at a boy who consistently earns compartment marks.

'Sir, it has no relation to my additional burden…Err… sorry, Sir, I mean the mess secretary appointment. I really need a break. I haven't been on leave for two months, and that's a long time,' I replied.

'Hmm, you feel two months is a very long time,' growled the CO. Then, he calmed down. The COs of our Army are well trained to hit many birds with one stone.

'Okay, you take ₹20,000 from the mess fund,' he said, still studying my leave application.

'But, Sir, I have my own money. I don't need so much money. I don't spend so much. What will I do with it?' I said, rejecting the CO's generous offer.

'Bloody chap, don't jump the gun! I see that you are headed towards Gurgaon. They have Booze Marts in Gurgaon that sell foreign booze at cheap rates. The canteen these days keeps only crap sub-standard whiskies. Thanks to Bira, one can't find a decent bottle in the CSD. Get a few bottles of mucking Johnnie Walker Black Label.'

I saluted and proceeded on leave. I did as I was told, and after the leave, I came back with a good stash of Johnnie Walker Black Label in my rucksack.

Our bigger boss, I mean, the *jarnail saab,* only drank Johnnie Walker Black Label. He was a truly great man and leader if his tastes were anything to go by. Only Black Label passed down his fat neck. The rest of the whiskies probably met a blockage. Many were the days when I, as a culinary-illiterate mess secretary, stood over the cook, exerting him to grill the chicken and fish properly. Although I myself had no idea what a properly grilled or sautéed chicken or fish looked or tasted like, I could tell a *bajra* roti cooked to perfection or a glass of milk coming from a proper *murrah* buffalo of my region in Haryana. But meats, fish, and fowl were *taamsick bhojan* as far as I was concerned. The *jarnail* came to our mess many times. Every time, it fell upon me to ask the great man, 'Sir, what would you like to have?'

'Ashok, my standard drink.' I felt ingratiated that the great man remembered the name of a piffling Captain like me. As they say, a man's own name is music to his ears. This made the *jarnail* an even taller role model in my young eyes that found even a Colonel to be a senior enough rank. A *jarnail* was some sort of an extraterrestrial king whose august shoes blessed the red carpet of our unit.

Every time before leaving the mess the *jarnail* would say, 'If any one of you chaps are in Delhi, do drop in.'

He was stationed in Delhi. Many were the times he inspected our unit, and many and heavy were my responsibilities of keeping our harem of booze in the mess bar safe and stocked up with Black Label.

One day, two of us Captains went to Delhi to take Part B exams. The *jarnail saab's* house was close by in Delhi Cantonment. Shankar was toying with the idea of calling on the *jarnail saab.*

He said, '*Yaar,* every time *jarnail saab* comes to our unit, he says, "Guys, you must drop in whenever you come to Delhi."'

I agreed with what he said, but his understanding of the issue was not correct. I tried to tell Shankar that such statements and endearments by senior officers are not to be taken literally. But Shankar was a straightforward chap, and once an idea lit up his mind, he had the habit of seeing it through.

So, one fine evening, we took an auto-rickshaw and reached the bungalow. Tall gates tightly shut with a sentry peephole accosted us. We rang the buzzer bell, and the face of a man appeared in a slit window in the gate.

'What is your work?' he asked.

We gave him our name and ranks and told him that we had come to call on *jarnail saab*. He slammed the window shutter, and we sat on the culvert. After ten minutes, the small window opened again. The man was surprised that we were still waiting.

'*Saab* is not at home,' he told us tersely.

I got up to go and gave Shankar a smile that said, 'What did I tell you?' Shankar was made of tougher metal than I thought. He walked up to the man looking through the window and said, 'All right, we will come again tomorrow.'

The next day, after giving the Military History paper, we wore muftis and again took an auto. At 7 p.m. sharp, we reached the bungalow. Shankar pressed the bell. The same man peered again and instantly said, '*Saab* is doing Pooja,' and slammed the window shut. If Shankar had an iota of diplomatic understanding, he would have understood that he had been effectively told to get lost. But Shankar's mind was composed of stainless steel. Nothing could bend him from his set purpose.

So, we sat at the culvert again. I bet a bottle of Black Label to Shankar that we wouldn't get past the gate of the bungalow. Shankar said that he would, at any cost, even if he had to jump the wall to go and call on our role model officer. He said that the lower staff always posed difficulties, but the General was a great guy.

We sat for half an hour, and then Shankar got up and pressed the bell again. The Rasputin again appeared in the window slot.

'Hasn't the Pooja finished yet?' asked Shankar.

'*Nahi. Saab* is doing the *Mahamrityunjay jaap,*' he again slammed the window shut.

Shankar came back. I said, 'Let's go back. We are wasting our time. We won't get past those closed gates. Don't get *senti, yaar.*'

After some time, as if the wishes of Shankar were heard by some divinity, the gates opened, and we both were ushered into a capacious drawing room. The General sat in an Adidas tracksuit with a cup of tea. He welcomed us with a warm smile. After some chit-chat, he said to the servant, '*Jao,* go and get two cups of tea for *sahab log.*'

Before the servant left, Shankar said, 'Sir, we don't drink tea.'

'Then what will you have?' the *jarnail* asked.

'Sir, the same drink that you have. Black Label,' came the reply.

There was pin-drop silence all around.

The *jarnail* turned to the flunkey and said, '*Jao*, go and get two Black Labels for *sahab log.*'

The flunkey returned after some time, holding an empty tray.

'Sir, there is no Black Label,' he told the *jarnail.*

'*Accha*, go and get some Teacher's 50 then,' the *jarnail* commanded. The flunkey disappeared and returned after some minutes, empty-handed, '*Saab,* Teacher's 50 is also not there.'

The *jarnail* huffed, '*Accha aisa karo, do* Blenders Pride *le aao.'* (Go and get two Blenders Prides.)

The alert flunkey came back after some time, looking crestfallen, 'Sir, there is no Blenders Pride either.'

The *jarnail* thundered, 'Okay, okay. I see. Go and get whatever is there.'

A moment later, the flunkey came out, carrying half a bottle of Old Monk rum.

'Don't mind, guys. Today, let's have a soldiers' drink.'

So, we had two pegs of Old Monk each and some Lays potato chips and came back to our room.

Bahar piyo whiskey,
Kadon iss di, kadon uss di.

Ghar piyo rum,
Dey danaa dan dann.

Noori

~

'"He had *fauji* cooking oil hydro running in his veins." I will talk about Noori only if you write this exact statement in your story.'

I agreed to write his exact statement, and that satisfied him. I had first met Senor Black Dog (BD) at the Allahabad Services Selection Board (SSB) Centre. Tall and elegant, he resembled the English actor David Niven. Senor was an open-minded and kind man without airs of *faux* superiority of any kind. He was appearing for the Indian Military Academy's (IMA) SSB, and I was a boy trying for NDA. Senor was a very affable and observant senior even then. He recognised me straightaway after a gap of more than 20 years. He was that sharp an officer. Then, we met at the club often and gassed away on the club lawns under the twinkling stars of the Milky Way.

'Who are the most loyal creatures of *fauj*?' asked Colonel Black Dog one such evening.

'The Chief of Army Staff?' I replied.

'*Nahi*,' (No) Black Dog shook his head.

'The Army Commander?' I tried again.

'Wrong,' pat came the reply.

'The Corps Commander?' I hesitated now.

'Negative,' he smirked.

'The Colonel of a regiment?' Honestly, I was running out of guesses now unless naming the ranks of officials was the question.

'Balls,' the Senor said haughtily.

'The Subedar Major?' I was at my wits' end.

'Tera dimag ghutne me hai, Jaat Ram,' (Your brain is in your knee, Jaat Ram) declared Black Dog as his considered opinion.

'Agreed, Sir, now please give your DS the solution,' I grumbled.

'It's the post dog that hangs outside the *langar*,' quipped Senor.

Black Dog was a brilliant infantryman, and he had the habit of poking his bayonet inside larger egos than mine.

He lit another Gold Flake and threw the next viva question, or that was what this seemed to be, at least.

'Who is the second most loyal creature of *fauj*?' asked the carefree man.

'The barman.' I tried my luck by giving an unconventional answer.

'Ha-ha, you are catching on fast, but wrong again,' he said, waving his hand to call the club bearer.

'Sir, I have no idea,' I (Old Monk) said, throwing in the towel.

Black Dog lifted his whiskey glass elegantly and took a sip, 'It's the post porter, who is a multipurpose handyman. He, too, hangs around the *langar*.'

Black Dog was in a philosophical and enlightenment-passing mood. The whiskey had oiled his memory, and the cigarette smoke had added a piquancy to his speech, like chicory added to coffee. He continued, 'Anyone who tastes food cooked in *fauji* cooking oil, oil hydro, becomes addicted to the Army ways. He becomes like a dog of the meat market; nothing can make him go away.'

Noori was newly married; his family had cornered him into marrying a girl of their choice. But even after marriage, he lived at an Army post where he had been working since he was a boy. He had accompanied his father, who used to work at the post. There, he had met a girl who used to live in a village close to the post. Their eyes met when he saw her grazing goats on a grassy meadow, and their gaze had remained locked since then.

A rare sort of date palm grew on the spurs of these pine-clad hills. The same rare trees grew on the next spur and then the next. There was a legend about these date palms growing among the Himalayan pines. These palms marked the line of Alexander the Great's outposts. The date clumps had descended from the dates Alexander's soldiers had brought from the Tigris. This was the farthest limit of his penetration. Even the names of places seemed genetically linked to the legend of Alexander, son of Philip of Macedon. The old hillmen whispered that Maendar Gali was named after King Menander, an Indo-Bactrian king who ruled around 155–130 BC from Sagala (Sialkot). Menander was believed to have died in the area while on a military campaign. Even the nearby village of Bafliaz had a Greek connection.

Bafliaz, it is said, is where Alexander's horse Bucephalus is buried. The oracle of Delphi had foretold King Philip, Alexander's father, 'O Philip, the destined king of the world will be the one who rides Bucephalus, the horse with the mark of the Ox's head on his haunch.'

Bucephalus was a black stallion with a large white star on his brow. Alexander had tamed him in a wager with his father that he would ride the wild horse of the finest Thessalian strain, who allowed nobody to come even close to him, leave aside ride him. A 13-year-old Alexander had managed to turn the horse towards the sun, jump on him, and ride him. Philip was so impressed with Alexander that he had said, 'O son, look for a kingdom equal to and worthy of thyself, for Macedonia is too little for you.'

Black Dog descended suddenly from the fourth century BCE to the twenty-first century CE: 'I was posted there as a subaltern upon commissioning. I came to know Noori well. He was our post porter. One cannot have a drink in the company of one's troops, but with Noori, it was different. I wanted to learn all I could about the area, its history, people, and the life of the people. At first, he said no to the rum or whiskey that I gave him to drink, but eventually, he started taking a drink.

'Our battalion's time finished, and another battalion came, and Noori was handed over to the next battalion. I thought that would be the last I would see of Noori. I lost touch with him and forgot him completely. 14 years passed, and once again, I found myself as the second-in-command of a battalion in the same area. My first search after I returned was for Noori. He was still attached to working in the *langar* and doing the major-domo's work. He had a few flecks of grey in his shiny jet-black hair. He was married to his second wife and had two robust sons.

'One day, a middle-aged Pakistani woman ran into India after crossing the LoC. She was brought to me. I asked her why she had crossed over into India and if she knew that it was illegal. She said that she knew the position of law, but she had come to India to escape from her abusive husband. The man had beaten her and mistreated her all her life, and she had had enough. One day, she just felt compelled to leave everything behind and find a new life. We insisted a lot that she should return to Pakistan. But the *buddhiya* said that she would give her life rather than return. What were we to do with her? I knew only one man who could be entrusted to look after her. She insisted that she would not eat even a single chappati if she was not given some kind of work to do. So, to Noori, she was entrusted. They could be seen working, lugging water, chopping vegetables, and doing the work of dog's bodies.

'After a few months, the battalion received orders to launch a transborder raid across the LoC. Although the news was very privileged information, the *buddhiya* got a scent of the raid being planned. One day, she walked up to my office with Noori and said that she wanted to have a word with me. She walked in and said straightaway, "Whatever you are planning, it won't succeed. There is nothing there."

'I was in a dilemma, whether to believe the intelligence inputs of the higher headquarters or the inputs of this old woman. I couldn't possibly tell the Brigade Headquarters, "Amina *bibi* says your intel is false."

'Anyhow, the intelligence from the *buddhiya* turned out to be true, and we were saved from being counter-ambushed. The whole operation would have been botched up had we walked straight into the trap.

'Many times, small people end up doing deeds that save many lives. This was one instance. The *buddhiya* who had come from Pakistan had repaid our kindness by giving us an invaluable warning that saved many lives. Noori, of course, was the catalyst of all things good. Who can forget such a patriot!'

'Sir, what was his real name?' I asked.

'Noor Hussain,' Black Dog got up and picked up his mobile phone and car keys.

'Now, when you write about him, don't forget to write that he had oil hydro running in his veins!'

The Leap of Faith

~

Now Romeo is beloved and loves again,
Alike bewitched by the charm of looks;
But to his foe supposed he must complain,
And she steal love's sweet bait from fearful hooks.
—Shakespeare, Romeo and Juliet, Act 2, Scene 5

Chamcha stood under the magnificent arch of the Red Fort's gateway. He was a man of medium height, but his flanks and the compact coiled aspect of his bearing spoke of activity. He was dressed in his Sunday best, brown checked trousers that fitted his sinewy legs like a hose pipe and a sky-blue shirt of good fit. He had pomaded his beard and twirled his moustaches to fine lancet points. The parrot green turban, very precisely done and tilted askance, gave him a rakish, devil-may-care look.

Chamcha was not his real name, and he stood talking to the man in charge of the gate—a guard whose name was Keemti. Even Keemti was not Keemti's real name. The Sikhs have a real name, but they pass their Army life addressed by their *nom de plumes*. *'O menu jaan do, tussi mainu jaan do, lo phaddo panjj rupiyey,'* (Let me pass. Please, here, take five rupees) said Sepoy Sohan Singh Chamcha to the guard Havildar, offering a five-rupee bribe.

5 Sikh was located inside the Red Fort, and the year was 1961. It was the Rashtrapati Bhavan battalion doing all the circus of military honour guards, guarding the complex, et cetera. 'Nothing doing. Piss off back. Come with a proper Sunday outpass,' said Keemti.

'But you have already allowed two chaps of Delta Company out without the pass. Anything wrong with my five rupees?' spat Chamcha.

'Who told you I have allowed anyone out? Don't bother me. As I said, bugger off. No outpass, no crossing these gates. Is that clear?' Keemti said with a hint of authority in his voice.

'Look, Keemti, it is of utmost importance that I go out today. You are from Faridkot, and I am from Kotkapura. That makes us almost brothers,' pleaded Chamcha.

'Nothing doing. Bugger off, will you? No outpass, no going out of the gate, and that's the law,' Keemti said, now irritated.

Chamcha took out a ten-rupee note and started waving it. 'A poor Sepoy offers you ten bucks. Please accept, brother. It's the maximum a poor man can spare,' he said.

The guard Havildar looked at Chamcha and smiled, saying, 'You never give up, do you? You son of a gun.'

'No, I don't. It's a matter of life and death,' said Chamcha.

The next day, the phone rang in the majestic grey stone barrack in the Red Fort. Captain Malhotra, the Adjutant, picked up the phone, 'Adjutant 5 Sikh.'

'Sir, it's SHO Banarsi Dass from Daryaganj Kotwaali on Civil lines. Shall I put him through?' asked the operator.

'Yes, do,' replied Captain Malhotra.

'Janab Captain *sahab*, Adjutant Sikh *paltan sahab*,' said the SHO.

'Speaking,' said the Captain.

'Sir, please send somebody to collect your man from the Kotwaali,' the SHO requested.

'I see. What's his name? What did he do?' asked the Adjutant after a pause in which he picked up a pencil.

'His name is...err...Sepoy Sohan Singh Chamcha and he did nothing. I mean nothing that is legally criminal, so to say,' the SHO hesitated.

'If he did nothing criminal, so to say, then why did he end up in your police station, SHO *sahab*,' wondered the Captain.

'Captain *sahab*, have you ever visited Gali Ballimaran in Chandni Chowk?' the SHO continued.

'I must confess I haven't gone there. The pressure of official duties leaves little spare time for frivolous pursuits,' replied the Captain.

'It seems that the Sepoys of *janab's* battalion have no such restraints working on their time. I won't blame Sohan Singh. Ferozaa has a penchant for *faujis*. Young *faujis,* that is,' chuckled Banarsi Dass.

'I am afraid I cannot make out what you are driving at,' said a puzzled Captain Malhotra.

'Sir, it's like this. Yesterday, our police party spotted a woman in the Delhi Gate Garden with a young Sikh,' Banarsi Dass supplied more information.

'So what? Is it a crime to sit with a woman in a public garden? I think that's what public gardens are meant for,' the Captain was amazed at the man he was speaking to.

'Yes, indeed, Sir. But in this case, the woman was Ferozaa,' said the SHO, hoping the Captain would understand.

'So what?' questioned the Captain again.

'Aaa, err, she is a woman with a bit of a record. So the police constables arrested her there and then,' sighed the SHO. This was taking more time than he expected.

'Then?' the Captain was at his wit's end now.

'Your man said that the woman was his friend, and she was committing no crime,' Banarsi Dass spoke.

'Then?' the Captain repeated himself.

'But we had to get her to the station. The Sepoy said that if his friend was to be arrested, then he would not mind getting arrested with her. In fact, he demanded that he, too, be arrested. Our constables advised him not to get entangled in the *ruffadd* (kerfuffle),' informed Banarsi Dass.

'Then?' the Captain felt like he was talking to a child.

'Then what, Sir? We got both Ferozaa and Sohan Singh to the Kotwaali,' Banarsi Dass huffed.

'I see. I will send somebody right away. Thanks for your concern, SHO *sahab*,' enunciated the Captain.

The next day, an unrepentant Chamcha was marched up to Colonel Bant Singh, the CO. 'So I've heard, Sohan Singh, you spent a night in the police station,' said the CO. The Sepoy kept silent. 'Sohan Singh, your name is not endorsed in the outpass register, and you did not have a Sunday outpass. How did you get out of the Red Fort?' the Colonel enquired.

Again, the culprit maintained a stony silence. The CO looked at the Adjutant, 'Looks like either the gate guards are not obeying orders, or the Sepoys have learnt to fly. Which of the two is it, SM *sahab*?'

'Sohan Singh, the CO *sahab* is asking you something,' coaxed the Adjutant.

'Sir, I jumped and went,' the Sepoy at last broke his silence.

'I see. Indeed, the Mughals built a fort that could just be leaped across. Just like that. You are lying, Sohan Singh. Tell us the truth. Did you bribe the guard Commander to go out?' the Colonel asked.

'No, Sir. I didn't. I jumped across,' the Sepoy maintained.

'And you expect me to believe that that is the truth?' huffed the Colonel in indignation.

'Yes, Sir. It is the truth,' the Sepoy kept up with his story.

'I see.' The CO seemed immersed in thought and then said, 'Can you jump again?'

'Yes, Sir. I can,' the Sepoy spoke.

'Okay, show us,' said the CO, pushing back his chair.

Chamcha started walking towards the eastern part of the fort. The large courtyard of the Diwan-e-Aam was crossed, and then the Diwan-e-Khaas came. He went to the riverfront of the Mughal palace and stood on the rampart. The Yamuna had receded further eastward, and it flowed silverish and shiny in the distance.

The CO looked down from the ramparts. The wall was far too high, and the ground was far too low. A man was courting death if he plunged.

But before the sanguine balance of the mind would assert, there was a cry.

'Bolleey soo nihaal!' and Chamcha was flailing like a green thing in the air. He crashed on the ground, rolled like a log, and lay still.

The tragedy was highly avoidable, thought Colonel Bant Singh, looking at the olive green man in the moat down below. The man in the moat moved, got up, and stood at attention.

Chamcha was again marched up to the CO the next day.

'Mallu, what do you think we should give him?' asked the CO.

The young Captain thought awhile, 'Well, Sir, for this offence, the standard punishment is 14 days of rigorous imprisonment in the quarter guard.'

'I see. March him in,' the CO commanded.

So Chamcha was again marched up to the CO. The CO looked at him long and hard and said, 'I promote this man to Lance Naik and from tomorrow, he will be my cane orderly. March him out.'

That's how Chamcha got his first promotion. But now, he was the poster boy of the battalion because only the smartest Sepoy of the battalion was selected to be the CO's orderly. His Sundays were off, and some say that Chamcha used to watch cinema with Ferozaa. It's not every day that one finds men who can jump down the Red Fort's wall and walk away.

The Government Dog

Cry 'Havoc!' and let slip the dogs of war.

—Shakespeare, Julius Caesar, Act 3, Scene 1

The dog was beautiful, and by the stern and unalterable laws of distribution, it went to an Assam Rifles unit in the northeast. The unit was nicknamed Seven Sisters' Military Dog Unit, SSMDU for short.

Frieda was a pedigreed German Shepherd, bred in the very hot summers and very cold winters in the kennels of the Army at Meerut. The dogs—Labradors and Alsatians—trained underneath the grand old peepal trees. Nearby, in the holiday home for retired Army dogs, the senior dogs drank milk and slept their old age away under the mango trees, having given the best years of their lives walking the roads and tracks of Kashmir, sniffing for explosives. Overhead, the brown-headed barbets kept up a loud monotonous *korr, kutroo, kutroo* call, almost incessant in summers—a time when the call of one barbet starts off others in the area, and the chorus continues.

When she did her basic military dog training along the old peepal-lined roads, Frieda drew an 'ahh' from the onlookers and dog lovers. Such was the limpid grace of her bobbing walk and the undulating slope of her back, which rolled down like a Gulmarg meadow to end in powerful hind legs. When she walked purposefully, it was with the pulsing grace of a pantheress.

She was the show stopper of SSMDU at the Annual *Pundra Agast* (15 August) Dog Show. The padded man, who had been selected for the demonstration of the dog's strength, found it impossible to shake her off his arm—nailed shut inside Frieda's jaw.

Soon, the drab and repetitive life of the small cantonment was rippled by good news. The Area Commander, Tambu Singh from Sainik School in Tambupur, kept his plastic Uniball pen down and picked up the log message book of the station that had a message from SSMDU. His red pen hovered over the much-used register, and he read the message again. It was from the local Dog Unit Commander, SSMDU, informing his bosses about the litter given by a German Shepherd she-dog called Frieda.

The fishnet of military bureaucracy is not any looser woven than that of any other branch of government service. Ours is the best file, register, and reporting service anywhere in the world. The report of Frieda's litter was simultaneously riding the radio waves of *awaan*[4] (AWAN) towards Calcutta and New Delhi headquarters. The telegrams were printed and stuck in relevant files, and diligent clerks updated the number of Alsatian pups on the feeding strength of the Army. The PowerPoint slides were also being purposefully amended, and overzealous and ambitious ZE (zero error) staff officers were

4. (Slang) Army Wide Area Network.

shooting off messages for the photographs of the pups to be shown in hyperlinked PowerPoint presentations. The modern-day staff officers of the Army are powerful hunters of zero error. They can spot and kill an error at three light years' distance.

The officer looking after the SSMDU was a dyed-in-the-pedigree-packet kind of a vet named Jambu Singh. He had grown up reading James Herriot, and he loved the world of animals. He took out a pink 2,000-rupee radio chip note and gave it to his senior JCO, Subedar Mulkmalik Singh, 'Please distribute laddus in the unit. Frieda has become a mother, and the arrival of the new pups must be celebrated. These are the first pups of the season,' said the blessed Jambu.

'*Ji hazur, bahut badhiya,* Sir.' (Sure, Sir, very well.)

Jambu tapped his mobile phone to change his WhatsApp Picture. He had a picture of the chest-cavitied Hanuman ji with Sri Ram ji adorning the centre. Just for once, though, he would put Frieda's picture there. He was minimising Frieda's picture when he saw Mulkmalik diligently noting the order he had given for the purchase of laddus in his green canvas notepad. He found the JCO's habit of slowly noting down everything pretty exasperating.

'*Sahab,* please explain the distribution of laddus,' said the JCO. Though it appears a simple enough task, in the affairs of humans, the distribution of favours—a cause for joy—can also become a gripe. The art of keeping everybody happy and feeling important often falls on the shoulders of the senior JCO.

'That I leave to you, *Sahab*. And also, please have a *mandir karyakram* (temple program) to thank *Bhagwanji* (God) for the auspicious new arrivals in the unit.'

In the evening, Area Commander Tambu Singh was sitting on the verandah of Rhino Cottage with his wife, Mrs Tambi. Tambu was a henpecked husband. He looked forward to sharing all the office *gup-shup* (gossip) with his wife and then jointly deciding on whom to tighten the screws and in what way. While Tambu would work to make the particular officer receptive, his wife would use her own channels of AWWA[5] and family welfare to lean on the wife of that particular recalcitrant officer. Together, they worked like a lethal pair of Brad Pitt and Angelina Jolie, breaking the resistance of every thorn in the path. Tambu was a super-efficient chap. His ambitions were mapped over many years in the future and led towards the misty slopes of at least a governorship of his state post-retirement.

'A few Alsatian pups frolicking in our lawn won't look bad at all,' said Tambi after Tambu had updated her about the new litter at SSMDU. She dreamt of making Instagram reels of the pups playing amongst her daffodils and pansies and chasing each other through the *gamlaas* (flower pots) of Rhino Cottage.

The next day, Tambu Singh turned his open gypsy with a fluttering pennant over its bonnet into the gates of SSMDU. Mulkmalik was sitting behind the OC *sahab's* office, smoking a *beedi,* when he saw the black gypsy with two stars swing inside the unit gates. Mulk hurriedly threw the *beedi* and stamped on it. He fished out a green cardamom from his pocket and bit it, hurrying to inform Jambu Singh of the Area Commander's arrival.

Jambu Singh was reading the Royal Veterinary College's Journal of Canine Surgery when he saw the silver-headed Mulkmalik barge into his office saying, '*Sahab, khatra aa gaya.*' (Sir, trouble has knocked our doors.) Jambu kept the quarterly down and picked up his beret and put it on. He walked out just as the Commander's gypsy came into the office forecourt.

'Sir, what an unexpected honour for our tiny unit!' he said, welcoming Tambu Singh.

---

5. Army Wives Welfare Association

Tambu was on a fishing expedition and had put on his most gregarious and friendly face mask. Jambu was fairly experienced in life and civvy street to assign purely altruistic motives to the Commander's visit. He suspected something was amiss.

The Commander cackled pleasantries for a few minutes, appreciating the smart layout of the unit. Mulkmalik stood at a respectable distance, trying to divine the purpose of the bada *sahab's* impromptu visit. A ZE staff officer from the HQ stood poised behind him with a notepad and a submachine gun, Pilot V5.

'*Yaar*, Jambu, give me one of the new pups that you have. It will add colour and vitality to Rhino Cottage, and I will return it after some time.'

The staff officer's pen flew over his pad as he noted the point. Jambu swallowed hard and said, 'Sir, the pups are too small to wean off. If you allow two weeks' time…' he tried to speak plainly.

'Right. That's alright. Okay, then we shall be off.'

Jambu let out a deep breath. Mulkmalik kept looking at his officer. He studied the worried face of young Jambu. The pups had been entered in the registers and noted everywhere. They were now combatants in the making.

Mulkmalik, who had spent more than three decades in the service, came close to his officer and said, 'Sir, there is one solution.'

Jambu was a drowning man who clutched at the straw.

'Sir, I will get a *sastaa* desi *pilla* (cheap ordinary pup) that looks like an Alsatian pup from the bazaar, and we will send it to Tambu *sahab's* house. All young pups look the same. It's when they grow up a bit that the differences become discernible.'

'I say, *sahab*, that's a very good idea,' said Jambu with the weight of the world suddenly lifted from his chest.

'But there is one thing, *sahab. Aap apni* posting *jaldi manga lo.*' (Please get your posting orders soon.)

'Why, *sahab*?' asked the puzzled OC of the dog unit.

'Sir, because a *desi pilla's* ears don't stand up like an Alsatian's.'

After two weeks that stretched as time often does on such occasions, Jambu presented the pup to Rhino Cottage and soon got posted to Sudan on UN Mission for excellent services in SSMDU. Tambu sent his thumping recommendations for the prestigious foreign assignment.

One day, I met my friend Tambu Singh. He had retired and was walking a beautiful desi mongrel to which he seemed very attached. Apparently, his dream of becoming the governor was fluttering like the discarded pin flag on an old sand model of a veterinary strike. Sometimes, he broke the monotony of life and went to TV news shows to talk about the Ukrainian war.

Mulkmalik has retired now. He has no specific use of dogs in his life now. He spends the evening of his life grazing buffaloes in the hot fields of native Haryana, where the hot winds blow restlessly throughout the day. Jambu Singh has become a kind of one-trick pony. He has perfected the game of ingratiating senior officers by presenting them pups and earning thumping annual confidential reports. As a reward for good services, he is recommended by his seniors to go with Indian Army contingents to various employments overseas for the United Nations Peace Keeping Forces. The pay is five times more. He is getting ready for his third UN mission posting.

The Trees of Subedar Singh

~

Our Brigade was located in a barren flatland, many miles out of town. The ground was as bald as a monk's head. Not a blade of grass twitched to the caress of the wind, and the scorching Indian heat beat a tattoo throughout the day, and everything baked.

One morning, a messenger came to me and told me that the Colonel, my CO, wanted me. I had just come from the IMA, and my uniform, as well as the uneasy star stuck on my shoulder, were new.

The CO was reading a file. He ignored me. I stood and rotated my eyeballs and took in the office. My eyes fell on a large sketch plan on the wall behind the CO's chair. He closed the file and kept it aside. Then, he rattled out a number of lowly jobs for me to do, as befitted a freshly-coined Second Lieutenant. Laden and weighed by a bagful of chores, I came out.

I walked into the cubicle of the CO's secretary and asked the NCO (Non-Commissioned Officer), 'What is that big chart in the CO's office?'

'That is the unit arboriculture plan. A tree plantation plan along with numbers and varieties depicted in different colours,' the answer came.

In the coming days, we got busy planting saplings. The emphasis was on numbers. Nobody seemed to be bothered to check if the trees we were planting were suitable for the soil and climate. With the tree plantation done, I got busy with other things like everybody else, but in the meantime, fate was slipping lead into the boxing glove.

One day, alarm bells went off in the unit. The Brigadier, who was the boss of my Colonel, was coming to see how the planted trees were doing. The CO called me and asked, 'How are the trees doing?'

'Sir, they must be doing fine,' I replied.

'What do you mean they must be doing fine? Hasn't anyone told you that you are the officer in charge of the plantation? Tomorrow, the Brigade Commander is coming to have a look. Before he comes, I will come and have a look myself,' the CO thundered. This came as a surprise. I hurried to the plantation area. Almost all the saplings stood wilted and lifeless in the dry earth. Once green leaves, now as dead as dry plastic. Only about one out of ten plants had survived.

I came back to my battery, bowed down by the impossible embarrassment in store for me. I called the battery senior JCO Subedar Singh and explained my predicament to him. He was a tall, dour, Viking-like figure. He heard me out and, without batting an eyelid, said, 'It will be taken care of.' Then, he turned and walked away.

The next morning, the Colonel came to the plantation in an open Jeep. He swivelled his neck 180 degrees and nodded. A whistle blast was heard, and the Brigadier's Jeep came in. He was a tall, handsome Armoured Corps officer wearing a black dungaree. He stood up in the open Jeep and tapped his thighs with his riding crop. He was known to be a conceited man who rode a high horse and held others in contempt. He was known to be finicky and a remorseless fault-finder.

I stood next to the very tall Subedar Singh. I am not a tall person. I felt like I was standing in the shadow of a tree. We didn't dare move. The black-dungareed figure of the Brigadier stood in his Jeep like Rommel studying his positions at Alam Halfa. He saw the neatly-positioned plants like well-positioned tanks of a troop. Then, he whacked his riding crop on his DMS boots and declared, 'Good show.' His Jeep sped away, followed by the CO's Jeep, in a cloud of dust.

I looked at Subedar Singh, my gaze full of questions and joy. He said, 'Sir, the job was done. You should be happy.'

'But still, I want to know how you revived all these dead plants in just one night's time?' I insisted. He motioned me to follow him. He walked up to the nearest plant and pulled it out and held it in front of my face. This plant had no roots. It was a freshly cut tree branch. He walked to another plant and ran his index finger on its leaves. He raised his finger and held it up for me to see. The finger was green and smelled of paint, 'Of course, we had to paint many dead plants green. Thankfully, our battery had a paint drum only recently collected from the ordnance depot.'

I looked at the tall man. He nodded and said, 'This time, we shall plant suitable varieties, and they will survive.'

This was one of my earliest military lessons in calmness and resourcefulness.

The Marble Cross of Ferozeshah

~

In Indian Army argot, it is called Firepur and Freezepur. A red frog-shaped Tata Indica had crossed Moga and ran towards Firepur. The air conditioner had packed up, and it was about three in the afternoon. A few miles ahead, the timing belt wore out and broke in the heat. The poor man's Merc foundered like an exhausted long-distance runner short of the finish line.

It was 8 June, and the loo ripped through the branches of the forest department eucalyptus on the roadside. The long-cropped wheat fields lay bare and baking in the 50-degree sun. In the distance, large blue silos of grain rose like an alien space station on the venerable hoary chest of old Punjab.

We managed to reach Ferozepur on the hottest day of the hot season. Like John Nicholson in 1837, we were accommodated in the Ferozepur fort. There was no Honoria Lawrence to welcome the exhausted travellers. But, there was a very similar garret-like room closed from all sides that John Nicholson occupied. Heat-maddened, we dragged our mattresses outside to the ground, splashed water, and lay under a starlit sky.

Exhaustion brought sleep in the early hours, and the thick walls of the fort around us kept radiating shafts of unremitting heat.

Harnam Singh was the oldest man in Ferozepur cantonment. He lived in an old tumble-down bungalow on Jhoke Road. The house had cracks and walls tilting askew. One reached it across a path over which the branches of thorn acacia waved and stung. He was turning the earth in his tomato patch with a trowel. He was born in 1922, and his father was Billa Ram carpenter, who had provided furniture on rent to the *sahab log*. He went inside the house and came out with a sheaf of old receipts signed by sundry captains of Ferozepur Punjabis.

He lived with Bittoo, his bald son, who had bloodshot red eyes. Bittoo only spoke of the days of his youth when he owned a Triumph motorcycle. He seemed slightly mad. He only spoke of racing BSA and Triumph motorcycles all the time, standing there incongruously in a torn shirt and dirty nylon track pants. He started bugging me for a military disposal Bullet in good condition.

Harnam Singh spoke English in clipped sentences. He spoke with the wavering slowness of age when the grip on memory is slippery. I took him to the Saint Andrews Church, nearby, which has a grey slate roof. The church was built in 1854. Next to it was a large cricket stadium with a dusty pitch.

'What used to be here on the eve of Partition?' I asked.

Harnam Singh peered at the ground and spoke slowly. 'I think there was a fenced garden with a white marble cross in its middle, thereabouts.'

He pointed at the expanse of the cricket ground.

Then, we drove to the War Memorial crossing on the Mall Road. Three-quarters of the crossroad circle had memorial walls in cream-coloured Dholpur stone. Names of soldiers of Ferozepur district who perished in the white man's war were inscribed on the stones. In one quadrant stood a white marble cross, about eight feet in height, carved out of a single stone.

'Is this the same cross?' I asked Harnam Singh. The tiny Sikh pushed his turban up over his brow, and I helped him get off of our Maruti Gypsy.

He walked to the marble column and examined it quietly.

'Yes, this is the same monument. I wonder who shifted it here to the Mall Road.'

On 23 December 1845, the British started ascertaining the extent of their casualties at Ferozeshah. Hugh Gough ordered all British war dead to be taken to Ferozepur for burial after identification. The wounded were also carted to Ferozepur.

'No British bones will be left to bleach in Ferozeshah.'

The mass graves containing about 800 dead were marked with a white marble cross. Later on, a church was built nearby as a memorial.

The Leopard Who Died of Shame

~

In a certain officers' mess of a Sikh battalion hangs the skin of a leopard, and under it hangs a brass plate with these words engraved upon it: The Leopard Who Died of Shame. This is the story of how this beautiful and speckled feline trophy came to adorn the mess wall.

War was imminent. It was the winter of 1971, and the battalion was bivouacked in Meghalaya jungles, just in the shadow of the East Pakistan border. The officers spent the day out on patrols. These were followed by lengthy debriefings and operational conferences. The discussions lasted well into the night. After that, the officers came to the solitary bell-shaped mess tent. This was the best place. They played bridge in the light of the kerosene lanterns, had a few drinks, and wrote letters home.

One night, there was a very long sand model discussion of plans. It was a chilly night. The meal got late, and the poor man whose duty it was to wash the mess utensils sat on an empty jerrycan, waiting for the meal to get over. He was a young lad from Haryana. His trade was *masalchi*. This trade is the appendage of the times when armies marched at 3 a.m. to beat the Indian heat. The *masalchi's* job was to prepare and light the torches to illuminate the camp. Now, his job had mutated to illuminating, cleaning, and shining the mess-ware.

He heard the roistering of the officers. Someone was playing the harmonica, and an officer, who was fond of singing, was singing a Sehgal number. Outside the tent, *masalchi* Pooran Mal sat and dozed. He felt like smoking a *beedi*. He was addicted to the bad habit. The night wore on, and the cicadas and crickets buzzed in the forest all around. The men had slept. The sentry coughed, and moonlight glinted off his naked bayonet. He got up and walked to the bushes. There were strict blackout orders. The flare of him striking his match flickered for a second.

It was past midnight when the officers left the mess tent. The Mess Havildar was a mini tyrant. He wanted everything cleaned and spick and span before closing the mess. Pooran Mal faced a pile of utensils and cooking vessels. He was sitting next to a water trailer tank. The hirsute Mess Havildar came and stood over him. He ran a hand over his rope like mouche and said, 'Well, Pooran Mal, your job starts now. I want everything spick and span by breakfast time. I am off.'

A sleepy Pooran Mal sat nodding in sleep and scrubbing the utensils with ash powder. A sooty lantern gave out yellow rheumy light. He threw away the meat bones from the pannikin. The water was cold. He wished the Mess Havildar had allowed him some hot water for cleaning. The grease would come off quicker. But the Havildar said that precious kerosene oil couldn't be wasted to give hot water to the *masalchi*. He was lost in his thoughts when he heard some movement behind him and then the sound of the crunching of bones. He noticed that a stray dog was eating the bones. He didn't even look back. He continued working, his fingers rubbing the smoke-blackened surfaces.

The dog finished chewing the bones, growled, and slithered up behind his back. Pooran Mal felt the animal's hot breath on his neck. He was washing the heavy ladle which the cook used to fry pooris. He got up and saw a beautiful fat dog showing him fangs. He thought about the different kinds of dogs they had there. He swung the ladle with force and whacked the dog hard on his head. The animal howled and ran away.

The next morning, the Mess Havildar shook him up, 'Come, the CO *sahab* wants you.' The officers were standing around something golden and black on the ground. A pang of regret ran through Pooran. He had only meant to shoo the dog away. He told the CO *sahab*, 'Sir, the dog was pestering me. I only tried to shoo him away. I just tapped him lightly.'

The officers started laughing. The poor man didn't even know that it was a leopard. The CO then said, 'Well, Pooran Mal, if you didn't kill him, then he has probably died of shame for having been mistaken for a dog.'

And thereby hangs a leopard tale.

The Cantonment Barber Shop

~

The wife said, '*Tumne paddhney to hain nahi,* newspaper *band karwa do.*' (You are not going to read these newspapers; might as well cancel the subscription.)

She looked at the cigar-like rolled-up papers lying on the black box diwan in the balcony. She picked up one paper and read out, 'Six Rupees. So many six-rupee worth of papers lying about. That is 180 Rupees per month. It's a waste.'

The noble desire to keep abreast with the happenings of the world has waxed and waned over the years. The world has remained as it was; only the military mule is growing old. These days, it's competing with the reading of a biography of P. G. Wodehouse by Robert McCrum and James Herriot's *Every Living Thing*. Literature is pushing the good old *Indian Express* in the pending slot. I have to do some quick thinking as a cadet does in front of a growling sergeant asking for his I-slip.

The wife is a great fusser. I make a show of opening a newspaper. She is domestic-minded and never admits defeat to dust. She potters about her plants and plans the daily orchestra of the washing machine. Then, the planning of food, victuals and the ceaseless round of the day.

I pick up a handful of newspapers and stuff them in my sling bag. A haircut is long overdue, and I have been thinking of going to the barbershop. I drive to the small *fauji* bazaar in the station. It's called *Suvidha Kendra*. I wonder why a compound name like 'Convenience Centre' is allotted to the good old bazaar. We have adopted American ways. They call a pavement a sidewalk. Modern trends are funny. I have lived to see a cantonment being called a military station. They say a military station is a cantonment with a wall and gates. But wasn't that supposed to be a fort? I have seen Batman being called a buddy. A Sepoy called an Agniveer. A field ambulance called a field hospital, and a car or a Jeep called a light vehicle. This is a fascinating hobby—the observation of linguistic trends.

As I swing the door of the barbershop, Ram Sen, the barber, is sprawled out on a barber chair and getting his hair and beard dyed by one of his scrawny underlings. On the TV above the mirrors of the shop, a Suniel Shetty movie is playing, and a long-haired Suniel Shetty is punching the hell out of a score of villains. He, too, needs a haircut, I think. I sit and open a newspaper. I have plenty of time. My eyes home in on an article on the Mughal Gardens being renamed as Nectar Garden.

An Army man (that's what a good old soldier, Sepoy or *jawan* is called these days) is lying redolent on a barber chair. One of Ram Sen's apprentices is running the clipper on the sides of the man's head. I open the paper and read Narayani Gupta's article and glance up. Ram Sen, who usually cuts my hair, is allowing the hair dye to soak in. The Army man's hair is almost done. He gets up and takes his face very close to the wall mirrors. He is wearing a Rajput Regiment white t-shirt. On the left side is the crossed *katar* crest of the Rajput Regiment. I know the station has a battalion of the Rajput Regiment. He stares at his face, lifts his fingers, and tries to comb the short hair of his crew-cut temple. Ram Sen's apprentice barber has really given the Army man's scalp the grindstone treatment. He yells, '*Haye, mere baal kaisa kata*!' (Oh God! How have you cut my hair!)

This Army man looks like he is from Maharashtra; his way of talking has a Marathi touch. But he is from the Rajput Regiment. He is perturbed about his hair. Another Havildar enters in olive green Indian troops. He has a hackled beret of the Rajput Regiment. He tells Ram Sen, '*Sahab ke baal kaatne chalo.*' (Come with me to cut *sahab's* hair.)

Ram Sen is now washing his beard in a basin. A special force's Army man enters the barbershop. He is wearing khaki suede leather boots and keeps a beard. He sits on a chair and takes out his mobile phone. I think a special force's Army man used to be called a Commando when I joined the Army.

On the television, a scene with Tom Alter is now playing. He is saying to an antagonist, '*Tumharey jaisey kayi kutton ki poonch mainey seedhi ki hai.*' (I have straightened out the tails of many dogs like you.)

Where have those great scriptwriters of Bollywood gone now? The sheer bonanza of hearing the dialogues of those days is missing from present-day cinema.

The Marathi Army man in the Rajput Regiment shirt is still muttering, '*Haye, mera baal kharab kar diya.*' (He has ruined my hair.) By his tone, he seems to be thinking if he should quarrel or not.

I return to the newspaper article about the *naamkaran* of Mughal Gardens. Evidently, the author has been walking the streets of Delhi since the 1950s. The article reads all right.

Having read the memoirs of Edwin Lutyens by his daughter Mary Lutyens, I learnt that the ground on which the Mughal Gardens stand belonged to Raisina and Malcha village—lands of Haryanvi agriculturists who were evicted by bringing in artillery canons to fire and raise the villages to the ground. The threat of a massacre made them vacate the land. Another interesting fact I read was that New Delhi was made at the cost of just one battleship of the British Empire.

The hackle-wearing Havildar, I apologise, Army man, again enters the barber shop, 'How much longer?'

Ram Sen says, 'It will take some more time.'

What I see is the absolute lack of urgency or stress in the three subjects in the barbershop. The special force's Army man is watching his mobile phone. The Marathi Army man of the Rajput Regiment is still scowling at his face and insisting that his hairstyle has been ruined. The hackled Havildar is sitting in a Safari outside. All seems to be well in the world. An Army man walks in with a little boy, 'Hish *ko katora cut de do.*' (Give Hish a crew cut.)

Ahh, the sound of Hish! This fellow has to be from Garhwal Rifles. I raise my eyes from the newspaper. But he is also wearing a Rajput Regiment t-shirt. I scratch my head. What has the world come to?

On the TV, Suniel Shetty appears with a haircut, but this time, he has forgotten to wear his shirt. He is pummelling the goons with a chest bristling with hair like the good old black barrack blanket. Now, even that has gone out of fashion.

Ram Sen is finally dyed and renewed, looking like a freshly painted black trunk of *fauji* people ready for administrative inspection. On the television set, after beating about 2,000 people to a pulp, Suniel Shetty is marrying his love interest.

Mr Ram Sen says, '*Aaiyey, apke baal kaatte hain.*' (Come, let's cut your hair.)

The Congenial Maid

Bertie Wooster and Jeeves in the Indian Army

~

'Shall you be wearing this for your evening walk, Sir?' asked Jeeves, lifting my neon Adidas t-shirt. He was dangling it from his index finger and looking down his nose at me.

'Anything the matter with it, Jeeves?' I asked.

'No, Sir. Only that now you are a full Colonel and that too time scale; someone might mistake you for a Captain, that too a short service one,' Jeeves replied.

Now, Jeeves always has a point, especially on the days when he has started the day with two tots of Contessa rum. Darn the man! He used to be quite in his senses when he drank half my monthly entitlement of Old Monk. Hang the CSD department for stopping Old Monk and putting out Mohan Meakin on the out-of-bound list of booze along with Glenlivet, Johnnie Walker, and Chivas Regal, and bringing in Lion Daddy.

The pure drop was not doing any good to Jeeves' usually unfailing common sense. Anyhow, I had to wear the same old white t-shirt, and out I went before he said something complimentary about my jet-black hair, which was the result of the Garnier hair colour that had replaced my favourite Godrej hair dye.

I stepped out for my evening walk. It was a fine evening, and the friendly bulls were rubbing against tree guards. A bovine herd of cows sat near the basketball court. They had been hanging out there since the cow kiss day, refusing to leave the officers' quarters, which made me think that they had become rather fond of kisses. I was wondering when the government would declare a dog kiss day since there were plenty of them sprawled out along the roads. My pleasant thoughts were punctured when I saw a young couple approaching. He must be a young Major, I thought. They were walking a sniffy pug dog that was stopping at every bush and roadside turd and sniffing with long, satisfying inhalations. The lady was wearing a skin-pasted Lycra legging that was not helping in hiding the fact that she did not go easy on the butter and cheese. I put him in the service bracket of eight or nine years when the first flush of seniority makes an officer comb his hair straight back from his head and carry a swagger stick when walking his dog. He was carrying a thick stub of a bamboo cane, which would be sufficient to keep a belligerent bison at bay.

I was wondering whether the officer and the lady would wish me first or whether I should wish them first. Notwithstanding the Garnier hair colour, I couldn't just hide my 30-odd years of service in which 15 had been spent in passing the infernal Part D exam. I was weighing my options like the Chief Justice of India weighing the appropriateness of the Supreme Court working under the Public Works Department.

Till a few years ago, a breezy 'good morning' or 'good evening' used to suffice between officers, and one heard the beautifully diverse greetings of the troops. I thought I would wish 'good evening'. I have a fair sprinkling of greys on my temples; of course, today, they were all camouflaged by Garnier.

The woman was wearing a tight spandex bottom, and the man was in some kind of red and yellow fluorescent shoes. I said a gentle 'good evening', but the couple went talking in what sounded like Swahili language to my ears. They moved on without taking any notice. The sound of my own greetings died in my ears like a stone disappearing into water. I made a mental note to ask Jeeves upon my return what could be the reason for the officer who walked the pug not returning my wishes.

There are a few regular stray dogs one comes across on one's walking route. Whenever I cross a pie dog, I mumble a silent prayer; this, again, was Jeeves' wonderful suggestion.

Bade bhai kaat na lena. Maine tera kuch nahi bigaada hai. (Big brother, don't bite me. I have not caused you any harm.)

The prayer seems to work swimmingly in most cases until one crosses the Brigadier's house. The philanthropic man always has two very fat pie dogs sleeping in front of his gate. They are the fattest pie dogs in this cantonment. Their health is fair testimony that, at least, the Army Service Corps is doing its job well and truly beyond the call of duty and keeping the medical specialist gleefully happy in declaring officers overweight. The rations lead to a marvellous gain in girth of both men and beasts, and at least, in the case of stray dogs, they bring the required aggressiveness of purpose, a high Officer Like Quality (OLQ) that is fostered in a military environment. I must share my accidental illumination with Jeeves once I get back from the walk.

The fat pair, as usual, was dozing in the sun when I happened to pass that day on my evening walk. They had dug shallow burrows and were keeping a watchful eye on the road traffic. Beakers of splashed milk and chappati crumbs lay nearby. When I approached the philanthropic Brigadier's house, the faithful pair fixed me with a malevolent glare and bared their teeth and growled. I wish I had a tail to wag at them and get the visa on arrival and pass onwards. The fat bitch got up with an angry lethargy produced by drinking a litre packet of Saras milk from the ASC supply depot. I extended my hand and showed it the latest passport I was carrying in the form of a big rock. It turned wisely and sat down in its burrow and looked at me like a bored bank watchman eyeing a hungry and skinny labourer who had come to open his *Jan Dhan Yojna* account.

Then, I was crossing a block of flats we call Majors' accommodation in our cantonment language. There is no minors' accommodation in the Army. These flats were of old construction in grey-brown Aravalli stone. The bare stone walls looked beautiful until some wisecrack suggested plastering them over with cement and painting them pink. Unfortunately, the pink distemper, like a lady's lip gloss, cannot last long. And so the cement-plastered and pinked-up houses started developing discoloured lines and scabs, looking ugly and unkempt. A few blocks had mercifully not yet fallen to the pinking and blended beautifully, peeping like stony homes from the branches of *gulmohars* and acacia.

A friend used to stay in one of the flats. Now, alas, the flats' plaster was quickly becoming green and grey. The MES does a wonderful makeup job that very soon starts vanishing, as good makeup should. The dear house lay vacant and already looked witch-haunted. The wings of memory took me to old times and that wonderful dinner at his place as I walked.

He used to have a very beautiful and young house help. She would cook and give company to his old mother, who used to live with him. And the *memsahib,* who was also a very charming and elegant lady, taught her manners. He had a vivacious and charming young teenage daughter who was also very beautiful and followed strict dietary fads like eating two broccoli salads in olive oil and having seven almonds soaked overnight in water for breakfast with a dash of vinegar. Since the maid was also a young girl in her twenties, the blossom of youth was also abundant upon her. Soon, the fact became apparent that the consumption of broccoli, olive oil, and almonds and vinegar had almost doubled. He asked his daughter, and she said, 'No, dad. I am having only what I used to have.'

He let the matter drop, being a fine, large-hearted man. The house help, who was already beautiful, started looking even more beautiful, radiant, and marvellous. She had a fine figure, and *memsahib's* old designer suits that the lady passed on to her fitted her perfectly, and her soft long hair, sharp aquiline nose, and long-fingered slim hands, which she painted in glittering ways gave her quite a chic appearance. Like all beautiful women, she prized her beauty sacredly.

Once, the lady of the house was away visiting her own parents for a while. My friend had invited a few officers and ladies for dinner and had called me as well. He had said to me with a wink, 'Come over, Bertie. It will be good fun if you want to escape old Jeeves' tyranny for some time. I am expecting a jolly good evening, eh.'

I had scratched my chin and wondered what he meant. Anyhow, I went with a customary wine bottle that Jeeves had packed helpfully in hessian cloth because he could not find the roll of floral paper wrap that my aunt had given me on my fortieth birthday. Soon, the guests also started trickling in. We were all sitting in his beautiful drawing room, which was full of officers and ladies, and the room was filled with laughter and chit-chat.

Kanchan, the house help, walked in, carrying a tray with glasses of water. She looked every centimetre an officer's wife. Suddenly, all talk died down, and there was a spoon-drop silence. Officers froze mid-sentence like they do on Siachen glacier, and the ladies gawped with open mouths like they do when eating *gol gappas*. Kanchan walked in quietly, a smile fluttering upon her lips. The officers all got up from their chairs in unison and outdid each other in wishing Kanchan most graciously and sweetly, 'Very good evening, Ma'am.'

One or two raw youngsters even managed to croak out a tardy and parade ground-like 'Jai Hind, Ma'am.'

I lowered my glass of Black Dog ordinary and looked at my friend meaningfully. He ran his index finger horizontally over his lips. Everybody was transfixed and looking at Kanchan, who looked intoxicating in *memsahib's* passed-on Ritu Beri suit with a deep cleavage, upon which the dim yellow light played a game of shadows.

Kanchan smiled demurely at everyone and retreated to the kitchen quietly. At such moments, I wish I had extra sensory perception. I wanted to hear what went on in everybody's mind. I imagine I heard the nearest matronly lady mumbling to herself, 'What a glamorous tart! Nobody has the right to look so hot. No Colonel's wife has any business looking like Nora Fatehi when most of us look like Smriti Irani.'

I turned my head to see another woman's reaction to the elusive Mrs Kanchan. She seemed to be having heart trouble over a Bloody Mary that she was toying with. She said to one of the young officers, 'During our days, youngsters were supposed to graciously ask the lady of the house if they could be of any assistance.'

The young Captain, who was a RIMC chap, being quick on the uptake, bounced up towards the kitchen where Kanchan was stirring a cooking pan. He asked smartly, 'Ma'am, any help required?'

Kanchan turned her head towards him and said, '*Nahi, koi madad nahi chahiyey. Aap jaa ke baitho, me khud sab kuchch dekh loongi.*' (No, I don't need any help. You go and sit, I will take care of everything.)

The youngster came out scratching his head and stood next to the lady who had egged him to go.

'What happened? You seem confused,' the lady asked.

At that moment, Kanchan came in again, carrying a tray of kebabs, and the officers again jumped and stood up and started saying 'Thank you, Ma'am, thank you, Ma'am' after picking up the snacks.

The congenial maid again withdrew into the recesses of the kitchen and started stirring the chicken curry hurriedly. The ladies talked non-stop of the upcoming ladies' club laments, unliterary festivals, and skeletons in the MES cupboards that were all falling off the hinges and rotting. Then, they started comparing their maids and what rates they quoted to peel potatoes and give massages.

The dinner was laid, and one lady asked my friend, Colonel Tony Sen, 'Aah, Colonel Sen, please ask Mrs Sen also to join us for dinner. She has been looking after all of us so much and has not come out of the kitchen at all.'

'Ma'am, I would be very pleased if you can convince her to join us,' said Sen, and looking at me, gave a wink.

Mrs Manocha, who looked like Smriti Irani's twin sister, stormed into the kitchen and, holding Kanchan by her slim wrist, tried to pull her out.

'Come now, Mrs Sen. Leave your pots and pans and join us at the table. You have done enough for one evening,' the kind lady urged.

Kanchan, who did not speak English said, '*Aap kya bol rahe hain, mujhey kuch samajh nahi aa raha.*' (I don't understand what you are saying.)

Mrs Manocha thought that she was taking the '*Hindi hamaari matra bhasha hai*' (Hindi is our mother tongue) fad too far.

'*Chalo bhi, Mrs Sen. Hamare saath dinner khao.*' (Come on, Mrs Sen. Have dinner with us.)

Mrs Manocha thought about where one could find such *pativrata sanskari* wife these days. She was astounded that the pollution of Western ways had not touched Mrs Sen.

She stormed out and announced loudly, 'Colonel Sen, please ask Mrs Sen to join us.'

Sen was a sporting chap. He said, 'Kanchan, *aa jao.*' (Come out.)

After dinner was over, Kanchan asked Colonel Sen, '*Sahab, kal subah kitney bajey aana hai?*' (Sir, what time do I have to come tomorrow morning?)

The gathering stood dumbfounded. Mrs Manocha was red-faced and had an attack of her sporadic asthma. A good-natured youngster escorted Kanchan to the door and said to her, 'You would really make a fine officer's wife someday. Everybody believes so. By the way, I am Captain...'

Jeeves refused to believe my story. He said that all my studying to pass the Part D exams had affected my mental faculties. Jeeves, I have seen, is mostly right about all things.

Lady Laa Dee Daah

My surname, Ahlawat, is common in Army circles. Last evening, we were under the high ceilings of the Whelers Club in Meerut. A coal fire burnt inside a Victorian fireplace, proper with andirons and grate, and miniature paintings on the fireplace panels. An adjacent glass cabinet displayed heavy silver crockery of the club that was not in use. Our host was telling us that one General Nambiar, who came as a Meerut sub-area Commander in yesteryears, stole all the paintings, crockery and antique furniture of the club. There was a metallic wall art over the fireplace. It showed a voluptuously-bosomed woman playing the flute as her mane flew about like disturbed snakes. I was marvelling at the legendary theft and pusillanimity of General Nambiar. The General sure was a lascivious and horny bastard. The replacement contract for the artwork was also given to his wife's brother by him. My attention was caught by the extremely articulated voice of a lady.

'Hello, I am Veena or Mrs Rattan Singh,' she walked daintily towards my wife and said.

'Hello, I am Ashi, Mrs Ahlawat,' my wife replied.

Veena was a peroxide blond with a porcelain complexion and perfectly beautiful features. She must have been a prima donna in her heyday. She had the kind of voice that only girls who have studied in Welhams or Lawrence School Sanawar have. The laa-dee-daah accent of posh class and money. A giant ruby hung from a diamond neckband. Her blue and wine-coloured satin *lehenga* was so resplendent that it reminded me of Rani Jind Kaur, the last Queen of Punjab.

I bowed humbly and stated my name to this vision of grace and all things beautiful.

'Oh, so you are Ahlawat?' she said gracefully.

I nodded.

'My mother was also an Ahlawat. A Gochhi Ahlawat,' the beautiful lady supplied.

My wife piped in like an overeager myna bird, 'Even Ashok is from Gochhi, Mrs Rattan Singh.'

I knew what was coming. A village connection among the Jats of Haryana becomes '*Accha, tum isko jaantey ho? Accha tum usko jaantey ho? Merey dada kaa naam yeh tha...*' (So, you know so and so? This was my grandfather's name...)

The lady with the laa-dee-daah Cambridge accent had an ideal audience now, 'There, you see that man in the maroon cap? He is my husband. He commanded the Central Tonga Horse.'

My wife and I nodded in an appropriately awestruck manner. 'What a great thing, Ma'am! Amazing, Ma'am, so impressive!' I made noises of appreciation.

'What about your family?' She turned the tip of her beautifully carved aquiline nose skyward and asked me.

But before I could speak a word after thinking about what to say, her refined Oxbridge voice spoke again, 'My maternal grandfather was Colonel Santra Lal. He commanded the 5th Jokers' Horse and also the 3rd Smokers' Horse.'

Again, I nodded my head solemnly. I tried to smother my laughter. The way she was pronouncing it—Jokers' 'Arse' and Smokers' 'Arse'.

I was about to open my mouth, but she nipped me again, 'You must have heard the name of my great maternal grandfather, Colonel Khota Lal Ahlawat. He played polo with King Edward V when the King visited India. Do you know he introduced himself as Prince of Gochhi? And then there was Captain Hooka Singh, who was General Wavell's ADC when he was the Viceroy.'

'Yes, Ma'am. I have heard of Captain Hooka Singh from Duffer's Drift Horse and Mule Lancers,' I nodded in acknowledgement.

'Oh, I see. Smart man. So, young lady, where are you from?' she said, turning to my wife, in a Shashi Tharoorian accent.

My wife's throat ran dry, and I saw her Adam's apple shift up and down her neck like a stalled lift.

'Ma'am, she is from Meerut,' I said, coming to my wife's rescue. I could see that she was a veteran of the battlefields of bloodlines.

'What about your family?' she asked me.

'Me? Ma'am, my father did a life term for theft and homicide. He was a truck driver. He used to abduct pretty girls and sell them to needy villagers. And my grandfather was also a bandit of repute. We call him Dada Jumna Ram Chor,' I quenched her thirst for knowledge.

My wife started coughing as she sipped her fresh lime soda.

Lady Laa Dee Daah had turned a puce colour and was hurriedly seen waving to another old dolly, 'Madhu, how nice to see you! When did you come back from London? How nice to see you!' She waved excitedly to the other permed lady and made a hasty parting from us.

I picked up my glass of beer and started contemplating

what other thefts had been committed by the plucky General Nambiar. As I just mentioned, theft was in my blood and was an interesting subject when the evidence glowered at you from the club walls. Some years ago, the really wonderful old paintings of the club had been carted away in the name of refurbishment and modernisation. Modern arty trash paintings replaced the precious old paintings. And that's how modern-day theft takes place.

Malka-e-Jazbaat

~

The man who ran away with the rifle was court-martialled. Dharan was the prosecuting officer. His younger brother was also in the Army and retired as Army Commander. Dharan called me to the courtroom for deposition.

'You are IC 26420 M, 2nd Lieutenant P. K. Handa.'

'Yes, Sir, I am.'

'Do you recognise this man?'

'Yes, I do.'

'Where did you find him?'

'I found him in village Shahpura.'

'Was he armed when you found him?'

'Yes, he was.'

'Is this the rifle with which he was armed?' he said, pointing to a rifle kept on a table in the courtroom.

'I don't know,' I replied.

'What do you mean you don't know?' snapped Dharan.

'I said, I don't know if this was the very rifle.'

'What do you mean?'

'I mean, I can't say if this was the very rifle. All rifles look alike.'

Dharan asked for 15-minute adjournment in court proceedings and said to me, 'Look here, Handa. Come outside with me.' We went outside.

He started bullshitting me left, right, and centre.

'Do you think you are bloody Perry Mason, the detective? You bugger, you think you are too smart and you can play tricks?' In those days, Perry Mason was a widely-read detective series in which the character Perry Mason used to save culprits by finding legal loopholes in cases. His characters used to walk out of the courtroom scot-free.

'No, Sir, not Perry Mason.'

'Then what do you think you are? Sherlock Holmes or Hercule Poirot, perhaps? Why are you refusing to verify that it's the same rifle?'

'Sir, all rifles do look the same from a distance.'

He considered it a while and said, 'Do you remember the butt number of the rifle?'

'Yes, Sir, I do remember the butt number.'

'Then why didn't you say so earlier?'

'Because you never showed me the butt of the rifle, Sir.' Every Army rifle has a butt number painted on its stock for ready identification, besides the factory machine numbers engraved on its metal parts.

The court reassembled, and the proceedings began. Dharan asked me again, 'Is this the rifle?'

I said, 'I am not sure.'

'Come and have a look at the butt of the rifle.'

I went and pretended that I was having a close look at the rifle and said, 'Yes, it is the same rifle. The butt number is the same.'

Then, some more such questions were asked, and finally, the runaway Sepoy was court-martialled and sent home.

'And, Sir, what became of the Havildar?'

'Well, you see? It's like this that Havildar Jagir Singh was the national 50 km walk champion. He had brought laurels to the battalion. He was quietly asked to put up his papers and discharged from service.'

After this incident in which I had tracked and nabbed the runaway Sepoy, our new CO was highly impressed with my capabilities. He didn't know the real me as yet.

One of the companies of our battalion was deployed ahead of the Chenab River towards the International Border with Pakistan. That is the place where the Chenab and Munawar Tawi meet and flow towards Marala Headworks. I think it was the Delta Company. The senior Company Commander had gone on a posting or something. The CO called me and said, 'Handa, although you are just a Second Lieutenant, I am sending you as Delta Company Commander. Any problem?'

I came to a perfect ramrod straight attention and executed a drill square salute, 'No problem, Sir.'

The other officers present there, like Major Pannu and Major Brar, smirked and nudged each other with elbows. The new CO had come from outside. He was not from the 5 Sikh. He had no clue what the real Handa was like. God bless his departed soul. Major Pannu was a great officer. We lost him in the battle of Chhamb in the 1971 Indo-Pak War. Our battalion faced the brunt of a Pakistani Division attack, but that's a different story which I will tell you some other time, and you must write down our story of the 1971 War from the horse's mouth one of these days.

To reach the Marala Enclave, we had to cross the Chenab in very old and dubious-looking civilian boats. They only had one paddle and a single oarsman. It was the summer season, and snow was melting in the Himalayas. The Chenab flowed quietly, but the current was furious and swift under the harmless surface.

Once I reached the company, I asked who the best swimmers were. Many hands went up. Then I said, 'Are you sure all of you are good swimmers? Because I am going to take you into the Chenab river to catch fish.'

I asked the same question again. Now, there were only two men who raised their hands. The rest had all chickened out.

I had located a safe stretch where we could catch fish. One day, I took a PEK (Plastic Explosive) bar and threw it in the water, and when it exploded, all the fish came out and floated. I sent my *sardar* in the Chenab with a sack. He started collecting the fish. All of a sudden, he lost footing and disappeared beneath the surface. I thought he had drowned and I would be court-martialled. Luckily, he came out and walked back, carrying the sack full of fish.

I started sending fish and black partridge to the battalion. The officers came to know that Handa had come into his true form. There were a lot of black partridges there. I used to take my Dyna Point 22 rifle to *shikaar* (hunt) every day.

One day, we were walking back from *shikaar*. I saw a beautiful horse grazing in the distance. One of my *sardars* said it was on the Pakistani side of the fence. We went to check and found that the horse was on the Indian side. It was a beautiful chestnut mare. We got the mare to the company headquarters.

My company senior, the Junior Commissioned Officer, came and I told him to manage the saddle, stirrups, bridle, etc. *Sardars* are very resourceful people and love horses. In a day or two, he got me the saddlery.

On the first day, I took her at a full-tilt gallop along the International Border. A Pakistani Junior Commissioned Officer shouted in Punjabi, '*Janab*, the horse belongs to Pakistan.'

I also replied in Punjabi, 'The horse now belongs to India, and specifically, to Second Lieutenant Handa.'

'*Sahabji*, it's our officer's horse. My *naukri* will be forfeited if you don't return it,' he requested from the other side of the fence.

'Which officer? I have never seen any Pakistani officer here since I came here,' I replied.

'Our Company Commander *sahab* comes here once a month and uses this horse to go around,' he pleaded.

'Too bad. You can tell your officer to come and see me gallop here every morning,' I boasted.

'*O sahabji, tussi mainu marwa ditta,*' (Oh Sir, you've gotten me killed) he wrung his hands.

The troops across were also Punjabi Muslims. We spoke the same tongue. I named the mare Malka-e-Jazbaat after the famous Pakistani cine star of those days called Nayyar Sultana.

So, my life was going great. I was shooting wild boar and black partridge. Riding my mare, Malka-e-Jazbaat, thundering in full gallop every day, and generally having a ball. And, of course, reading a lot of Perry Mason.

This perfect idyll came to an end when my CO learnt that I was mostly decimating wildlife throughout the day, doing an MA in drinking and eating, and having a royal ball while horse riding and swimming. Who can digest such happiness of others? The order came for me to return to Battalion Headquarters. I had been in the Chenab Company for just three months.

'What did you do with Malka-e-Jazbaat?' the man I had been narrating the tale to asked.

'Well, you see…she had come from Pakistan. That was her true home. It was only right that I should return her to her country. With a heavy heart, I took her to the fence, and after giving her a last *thapki*, let her run free into her country.'

The Well-laid Plans

Bertie Wooster and Jeeves in the Indian Army

~

'Have you read this signal, Jeeves?' I asked, flinging a piece of paper towards the kitchen slab. Jeeves was busy cracking an egg to make my breakfast omelette.

He poured the mix into a pan and picked up the slip of paper. He read it twice and said, 'There is some mistake. It can't be true. Who has made you a Corps Commander? There has been some ghastly mix-up at Army Headquarters.'

'What do you mean, Jeeves? What the Army needs is exactly the kind of officer who can plan long-term strategies and, in the end, emerge victorious. I am sure someone has taken notice of my long campaign to pass the Part D exam. Remember, I took 15 years to overcome that enemy, but finally, I did. The minister is a great guy—only a real Frederick the Great can produce a von Clausewitz like me. He always knew I had the makings of a Field Marshal Montgomery and General Sagat Singh in me. Finally, someone has made the right decision. Go to the nearest *baniya* and get me a General's rank badge and make sure it's made of pure Ludhiana brass instead of the cheap Chinese plastic rank badges he palms off to gullible officers.'

'Now, don't you become too ambitious, Sir. You have that far-away look that hints at you having now set your eyes on the chair of the Army Chief. General Bertie Gangaram Govindrao Wooster, ADC, ABC, Order of the Black Sheep, Garter of the Grey Goose. I am sure they will detect the faux pas by evening, and you can go back to enjoying your study leave.'

As I know, Jeeves is mostly right, but it was the day of the summer solstice, and for once, I was triumphant. A signal did come, but only to confirm that I had been appointed General, commanding a very large corps in the Northern Command, which was called the *Kala Murga* Corps because it had a black rooster as its insignia. What a piece of auspicious good luck. Wooster in charge of the rooster. 'Ahh! Do you know how many soldiers will be under me, Jeeves?' I said.

'I hope none, Sir. Those kinds of things are prohibited in the Defence Services regulations. Alan Turing got chemically castrated for that sort of thing,' trolled Jeeves as he flipped the omelette in the pan.

'I must start writing my special order of the day that I will release on taking over the Black Rooster Corps. Bring a quill and ink,' I told Jevees.

Jeeves took out a Reynolds ball pen from his shirt pocket and handed it to me.

'What is this white straw-like thing? You don't expect me to write a momentous message with a cheap six-rupee pen, do you? Go to my table and open the drawer. You will find a gentleman's pen in there—a black Conway Stewart fountain pen. It was a gift from my grandfather,' I order.

Jeeves got the ancient ebonite pen, and I carefully unscrewed the cap, fixed it on top of the barrel of the pen, and started writing and speaking aloud, 'Ladies and gentlemen of the Black Rooster Corps, your prayers have been answered, and I am glad they had to choose me, Bertie Wooster. Cometh the hour, cometh the man. All of you are granted one-month French leave while I ensconce myself in the Flagstaff House. Then, we will start with a bang and a pop, like the pop of opening champagne. Good luck to all.'

'How does it read, Jeeves? Impressive enough, ehh?' I ask Jeeves after I have read the order aloud.

'Sounds as if your Corps will be on a permanent holiday spree after reading your special order of the day. I say, my lord, you must mean business; a no-nonsense message for everyone to pull up their anklets would be better, and no French leave. That kind of thing will upset all the housewives and make you very unpopular,' Jeeves requests.

'Jeeves, you remember that course I did in Army War College on the integration of artillery, infantry, and armour? The one in which I made the artillery lead the advance into Red Land and Nark Desh for a change and made the Ordnance and ASC chaps do the infantry's job and do *dhaawaa*? Well, that was much appreciated back then, and a special course grading was coined for my work called SG. Now, I bet you a bottle of Dom Perignon champagne if you can tell me what SG stands for,' I was confident Jeeves didn't know.

Jeeves flicked a stray strand of hair back on his imposing forehead and said, 'It's very simple. They gave you the grading called "Simply Great". You are not the first chap to have obtained this grading. Many before you have been anointed as simply great. Thou aren't a pioneer in the gallery of the Simply Great men of the Army,' Jeeves replied.

That afternoon, to savour the last few days of my anonymity and freedom, I, General-in-waiting of the *Kala Murga* Corps, strolled down to the CSD on my Kinetic Honda 4G scooter. I wanted to replenish my stock of Maggi noodles, Almond Drop hair oil, and Godrej hair dye and breathe the air as an ordinary officer. I belonged to that disappearing generation that smiled and said 'hello' to everybody, read the MRP labels carefully with the CSD price, and mentally noted the difference.

A young signals lady officer with her young male officer in Bermuda shorts and round neck t-shirt were strolling in the CSD compound. He smiled and said 'good morning' but received ice-cold stares in return that are reserved for unwanted salesmen selling LIC policy and people walking their dogs in front of your house.

I came back to the house feeling as if I had been bitten in the leg by my best friend. I told Jeeves about the CSD incident. Good old Jeeves could analyse everything clinically.

He said, 'I have been keeping a tab on your WhatsApp feeds in various groups. I think wishing seniors is a colonial baggage practice. A cold, hard stare is what is encouraged and appreciated nowadays that literally announces in capital letters—Mind your own bloody business; you aren't writing my ACR.'

The Man Who Loved His Splinters

~

Vox emissa volat; litera scripta manet.

(The spoken word flies away; the written one remains.)

The sun shone over the Arakan hills. The hills looked harmless and newly greened after the monsoons. The latest model of the new race of yellow-faced, buck-toothed men who had come to conquer India was stuck in these green hills. They had gnawed and snapped and charged at the eastern gates of India but were halted in the battles of Kohima and Imphal. Now, it was the defender's turn to hunt the wolves at the house gates.

A Sepoy sat on an upturned water can, peeling old potatoes—shrivelled like the flesh of old people. He was a hard-working young man of a quiet and sincere disposition—the kind of man who did his job quietly, thoroughly, and timely.

Such men are the boots of the Army, carrying the behemoth machine of war on their tender, tattered shoulders. Like other machines, this machine, too, was in need of rest, sleep, food, and hope. He saw the Dakota planes to the west behind their battalion line—white parachutes falling like snowflakes. The replenishments were being air-dropped. The man wondered if, along with the potatoes, onions and tinned food, the letters from home, too, had come. As the dead potato skin stuck to the dirt-laden nails and fingers, the man's mind meandered.

The war had come at a golden time for him. It was his God-gifted chance to break the family's cycle of debt. The dry rattle of poverty was all he had ever felt. So, he had told his father that he was going to get enrolled—there were a lot of vacancies, and they were calling for volunteers. He was past the age of recruitment, but those were the certificateless days. He had gone and stood in the mile-long recruitment line. He was fit and strong from all the farmwork he had done. Now, his pay was going to his father. Nobody needed money here in the Burmese jungles. He was happy with the *sarkar*. His father had cleared off the family debts.

He felt like he was living a charmed life. He saw the crows sitting on the mess tent, waiting to investigate the heap of potato peels and onion skin. The November sun felt warm—a thick shawl on his bare skin. He sat in khaki shorts and a white cotton vest, working in the mess. He didn't mind the work at all. In fact, he looked forward to the different duties—sometimes, caring for the sick in the long field ambulance tent, sometimes, going on patrols into the jungles to spot and fix the presence of the Japanese.

One day, he had been sent with a squad of Army propaganda team with loudspeakers, into the jungles, towards enemy positions. He had been puzzled at the site of those loudspeakers and batteries that he and the others had to carry. Then, from a guarded place facing the Japanese lines, the loudspeakers were laid. The Indian officers and NCOs started exhorting the spirits of the forests, it seemed. Who was going to hear them?

'Surrender to the nearest unit, and you can go home. No harm will come to you. We know you switched sides to survive the hardships and the torture. Do not fight your Indian brothers. You are fighting for a side that does not wish you well. The Japanese *sarkar* has no real love for you.'

These educated men moved all along the forest, blaring from their speakers at the enemy positions. When he came back, he was told that they were not to talk about what they heard and saw with anyone else. If they did, it would be a punishable offence. Then came word that their CO *sahab* would now be a Hindustani officer. All their *Angrez* (British) *sahab log* would be replaced by Hindustani officers. But the Sepoys knew that it made no difference to us. We were the ones who were meant to take bullets on our chests, no matter the skin colour of our officers. All of us knew that independence was around the corner after the war. That is why our own officers were being given high positions in the Army now. But if any new conquerors came to rule India, then it might take another hundred years to get rid of them.

Fairley *sahab*, our Angrez CO, was on his way out. There was a hill overlooking our battalion line at Razabil—a Japanese stronghold. The last order Fairley *sahab* gave was for the capture of this hill.

I was peeling potatoes in the officer's mess when my platoon Havildar came and shouted for all the chaps of my company to go and get ready. We were all issued two hand grenades and a hundred rounds of bandolier ammunition for our rifles.

There I was, working in the mess, studying the gently drifting parachutes, and thinking of home. And the next moment, here I was, all trussed up with a tin helmet on my head, ready to move off towards the hill held by the Japanese. The enemy position had sheer vertical sides, and they had taken great care to select an impregnable spot. The only approach was from a narrow ridge up a sheer slope. The platoon climbed up on all fours, helping and pulling each other up into the wooded hillside.

Mine was the leading platoon, and I was in the frontmost section. The enemy was cleverly camouflaged; no one could make out where they were. Machine gun fire tore through the jungle, and I felt the hot velocity kick of bullets in my left shoulder and legs. Hell, it was all so sudden! I was flung to the ground, and I breathed out the name of Ram. I looked around; I was seeing my comrades fall. They lay red, dead, and hot as freshly torn stone. I felt my soul tugging in the cage of my flesh, squirming to quit and fly away.

The enemy was raining fire, and the machine gun was spitting. The rest of the company behind us was pinned down the slope with Zorawar Chand Bakshi *sahab*, the officer who was with the attacking men. The Japanese came out of their trenches to investigate the dead bodies. I knew what would happen if they saw that I was alive. I closed my eyes and lay still, surrounded by dead men. As it is, I was wounded all over, soaked with blood, and in intense pain. Seeing blood oozing out of the corpses, the Japanese soldiers went back to their positions. I started crawling slowly towards the machine gun nest. When I was five yards short of the enemy, the Japanese saw me and threw grenades at me. One of the grenades went off in front of my face. More pain erupted in my tattered frame. This time, I think my face and chest were peppered with fragments. I pulled the pin from a grenade I was carrying and hurled it into the machine gun position.

When I dragged myself up to the machine gun, I found that its crew was all dead from the explosion. When the enemy realised something was wrong, they came out of the trenches, charging. I turned the machine gun on them and fired. Then, I think I passed out from the loss of blood and weakness.

The rest of the company had attacked by now and captured the hill. Bhandari Ram was discovered lying on the enemy machine gun position, more dead than alive. The position was littered with dead enemy soldiers. He thought he was going to die. He asked feebly, 'Is the objective captured?'

He was assured that the hill had been taken.

'Then I can die in peace now. I have done my duty.'

He was carried back, and nobody thought that he would survive, but survive he did. First evacuated to Calcutta and then to Bareilly Military Hospital.

Captain Zoru Bakshi, who had led the action, recommended Bhandari Ram for the award of Victoria Cross. Major Mohammad Usman, who had been the officiating CO under whom this action had taken place, also signed the VC Award citation. But in the meantime, 16/10 Baluch had gotten a new CO, Lieutenant Colonel L. P. Bogey Sen. Bogey Sen endorsed the citation but demoted the Award to Indian Order of Merit. Major Mohammad Usman told his CO plainly that he could not lower the award. Bogey Sen countered, 'IOM is no less an award.'

Major Usman said, 'Maybe so, but Bhandari Ram's action was a VC action.'

Maybe Bogey Sen was trying to show everyone in the battalion that he was now in charge, and his word was the last word.

Usman told him that since he was the temporary CO when the action took place, it was his recommendation that mattered and not Bogey Sen's. Sen said, 'Nothing doing.' But he had underestimated the moral nature of Major Usman. Usman went straight to the Brigade Commander of the 51st Brigade, Brigadier Thimmaya, and explained the matter.

'Sir, either Bhandari Ram gets a VC, or here is my resignation. Sen is nobody to change and downgrade the citation initiated by Zoru and approved by me, the then CO.'

Thimmaya, of course, the great man that he was, also agreed that the VC was the proper award for Bhandari Ram.

Captain Bhandari Ram *sahab* lived to the ripe old age of 87 years. At enrolment, his age had been recorded as five years younger. In old age, the shrapnel and metal fragments embedded in his bones used to stand out like chickpeas under his scars and skin. His sons used to wash their father's feet in prayers. The metal fragments were all over the legs, face and chest. One day, his son came up to him and said, 'Father, medical surgery has advanced a lot. If these shrapnel pieces bother you, we should have them removed.'

Captain Bhandari Ram Nadda replied, 'No, son. All these splinters are a part of me now. I feel a deep affection and loyalty to them.'

Post Scriptum

1. 16/10 Baluch Regiment was disbanded. Brahmin Dogras were allotted 8 Dogras after Partition.
2. Brigadier Mohammad Usman died at Nowshera in the 1947–48 Indo-Pak War. His funeral cortege was attended by both the Prime Minister and the President of India. He is buried in the Batla House graveyard in Delhi.
3. Bogey Sen and Zorawar Bakshi rose to high ranks of Army Commanders. Thimayya rose to be the Army Chief.

The Cost of Salt

~

'These *sangars*[6] can't stop the Chinese. They have already destroyed so many posts,' grunted a fair soldier from Jammu, who kept a pencil-thin moustache.

'You are right, brother. Janaki Das, what can we 23 men with old rifles do when the enemy comes with a whole *paltan*?' wondered Bhandari Ram.

Another man fighting to light a Panama cigarette in the cold wind reported, 'I have heard that first the enemy rains the post with mortar bombs and then attacks with automatic rifles.'

The conversation floated in the air. In a nearby hole in the ground, a radio operator kept trying to coax his radio set to life.

They had been trying to get in touch with their company headquarters for two days now. Earlier, they had heard on the

---

6. A low wall made of piled stones in rocky terrain, where digging in the ground is impossible. It is not a very satisfactory defensive construction, but still better than being absolutely in the open without any shield or protection.

radio set net that the enemy was advancing in their area. Other far-flung platoons had fallen. Soon, it would be their turn.

'Why should we stay here? There is nothing to defend here. Look around. Nothing but miles and miles of emptiness,' said another man who had lit a rag soaked in kerosene oil. He was desperately trying to warm his frozen feet. His ammunition boots lay to one side. They were almost brown—the top black leather skin worn and flaked away.

Thondup, the Ladakhi soldier, was chewing a rock-hard nugget of *churpi* (yak cheese). He stood with his hands in his pocket, his balaclava pushed back high over his forehead. He idly listened to the banter of his comrades, wondering what was going to be their fate.

Subedar Gulab Singh of the Jammu and Kashmir militia emerged from the wind-disturbed tent and called out for the platoon Havildar Hansraj. Hansraj was playing cards. He dropped his hand, got up, and came to the Platoon Commander.

'Yes, *sahab*. Have you decided then?' he asked the Subedar.

'What do the men say?' the Subedar countered.

'The radio set is dead,' came the answer.

'Yes,' muttered the Subedar. 'Last orders?' asked the Subedar loudly.

'No certain orders,' replied the Havildar.

'Look around you. Do you see any signs of relief or support? Anything for miles? We will all die here, and our bones will bleach for a hundred years,' complained the Subedar.

'The men want to do a *bada khana* and then retreat to safety,' the Havildar announced.

'Okay, then, we will have a *bada khana*,' the Subedar agreed.

'Now?' the Havildar asked, just to be sure.

'Right now,' the Subedar confirmed.

'Then?' the Havildar prodded.

'*Pitthu* on the back, rifle on shoulder, and *tez chaal* (quick march),' the Subedar sighed.

The *jawans* were happy to hear that they would retreat. They had been cut off—out of communication for many days. The Chinese were about to come and decimate them as they had done to other posts.

The platoon ate hurriedly, and the Havildar gave two tots of brown, chest-heating dark rum to all. They were ready to move. The Sepoys started moving in a single file. Gulab Singh saw a lone figure still standing at the post. Others had moved down the slope. He walked back.

'What's taking you so long, boy?' he asked Thondup.

'I won't leave the post,' said the Sepoy.

The JCO looked at him calmly, wondering how much rum the young Ladakhi had drunk.

'It's all right, come along. Everybody is waiting,' said the JCO patiently.

'No, *sahab*, I have eaten the salt of my country, and I can't leave my post,' replied Thondup.

'Are you drunk or what? Come along!' thundered the JCO.

The Sepoy stood there, adamant. The JCO thought that he would join up with the column as his rum wore off. He shrugged, turned, and walked away. And the platoon column withdrew from this post, which was ahead of Daulat Beg Oldi.

The Chinese Army withdrew in November 1962 after declaring a unilateral ceasefire. That year, the snowfall was heavy. For six months, the mountains lay under deep Arctic freeze. Blizzards and high winds lashed the vacated post. Snow fell every day, and the sun disappeared for many weeks.

The summers arrived, and bar-headed geese from the Tundra and Siberia flew over the evacuated post and descended near it for night's halt. The ice melted and sluggishly slid down the gullies. Moss appeared on wet rocks.

A foot patrol of the Indian Army was moving. The Captain, a curious *sardar*, asked his senior Subedar, 'I say, *sahab*, didn't we have a post of ours in this area before the Chinese came?'

'*Ji janab*, we had it over that knoll on the horizon,' replied Subedar Gulab Singh.

The *sardar* Captain leading the long-range patrol said, 'Okay, *sahab.* We will head there and halt for the night at our post.'

The line of men climbed up the scree slope. Rocks fell and slid as the party moved up. There was nothing much left of the post. The *jawans* who were carrying the stove and panniers entered a hole in the ground covered with green old canvas to make tea. Suddenly, they turned and ran out, pursued by a long-haired and long-bearded wild man, who came stumbling behind them, waving his bayonet and rifle. The wild man's hand and feet were swaddled in filthy rags and sacking, tied with telephone cable JWD.

He stared at them with hostility and stood blinking in the sunlight. All the men of the patrol stood frozen. Had they seen a God or a ghost? Gulab Singh was the first to regain his senses. Beneath the matted hair, the shape of the nose and forehead seemed disconcertingly familiar. His head swam, and he stood unconscious for a few moments. Then, he said, 'Is that you, Thondup?'

The Ladakhi soldier nodded his head. He was still manning his post.

A Bridge in the Dark

~

The tank chains were grinding and clashing as it pushed through the forest of tall reeds. The reeds grew up to the height of an elephant and popped like kids jumping on balloons on all sides as the tracks gnashed and clashed. The other tanks followed the dark shadow of the first tank that was creating all the fireworks of sounds. A man stood on the tank cupola, supporting himself by holding the machine gun on the turret. The tank tilted and slid like a seal as it negotiated a wide irrigation ditch and reared up on its tracks like a steed. The men, packed like sardines on the tank, clutched each other as two of them tumbled down. They got up, snatched their rifles lying in the sand, and ran behind the furious tracks of the tank. After some clumsy attempts to climb up the running tank, they were pulled up by eager arms. They started patting the web pouches they wore on their belts to see if any of their ammunition magazines had fallen out as they fell. They were all covered in sand. The CO, who stood on the cupola, told the men to run a pull-through in their rifles' barrels once they jumped off the tanks.

He returned to peering into the darkness. It was impossible to be sure of the direction. Not a single star glimmered in the sky. Winter haze and low clouds stretched overhead like black canvas. The tank's driver, whose hatch was open, squinted in the darkness and looked up at the man standing above him. The man above pointed his arm as if it were the needle of a magnetic compass. Having taken the bearing, he moved the stick to adjust the direction and pressed the pedal. As far as he could do, he had just been driving blindly, tunnelling into the *sarkanda*. They were driving along the shoreline of the Ravi river. The river flowed sluggishly and reduced in the month of December. The water in the Himalayas had frozen. They were keeping to the dry edge of the water, and when the driver suspected the ground underneath was softer, he would edge away, trying to avoid the water.

The *jawans* were silent as men who become quiet when they smell real danger. Many of them had taken small measures of spirits. The warmth of the rum took away their fatigue and gave poise to men who felt the illusion of immortality. Other people got killed, but not them. The tank kept pushing its great steel body onward, and the sharp leaves of the grass slashed across the cheeks of a man sitting above the tracks. He was about to mouth a curse when he cut the abuse rising in his throat midway. He realised that his CO was standing on the tank and it would be bad form to curse in his presence. He felt blood trickle from his cheeks and whispered to the other *jawans* to watch out for the swishing reed blades. The tank changed gears and turned a bit, throwing up clouds of sand that drenched all the men. They screwed their eyes shut and covered their noses and mouths. Partridges living in the grass took off in a whirring of wings, giving off loud bell-like sounds of anger and alarm.

The man standing on the growling tank that moved with a loud clashing of its track teeth and the angry breath of its diesel engines wondered if he was taking the right course. For how long would the tanks wheedle and plunge through the marshes around the river? How far was the bridge? The night was blind. A clod of wet earth splattered his face. He leaned forward to tell the driver to keep to the leftmost edge, then doubted whether the driver had heard him. Doubt, self-doubt—that was what he had to capture. The driver's head was covered with a tankman's rubber helmet. He knelt and thumped the man on the head. The driver eased the tank and stood in the hatch to hear what the officer had to say.

'Move a hundred yards to the left. I feel there is a marsh ahead,' The officer repeated his words, trying to speak deliberately so that the driver could hear him above the throb of the tank's engine.

The latter nodded his head and sank into the hatch. The tank coughed loudly and belched, its tracks squealed, and with a mighty jerk, all forty tonnes of it started turning and tearing through the mud like an angry hippo. The tanks following close behind also turned and started moving in the churned ruts of the leading tank. The other drivers shifted to drier ground and avoided moving on the churned earth, as the leading tanks had sloughed off the thicker crust of the earth, and tanks following in their wake started sinking to their belly floor. Soon, all the tanks were stuck in the marsh. The infantry jumped off and stood in small rings, hoping that the attack would be called off. Then, they were sent off to cut the elephant grass to ballast the tank tracks. The tanks were growling all about him as their steel tracks slid ineffectively on the bogey wheels.

'Damned bad luck!' cursed the CO silently.

He radioed the Brigade Commander, who played non-commital, 'Your baby, I will have no part of it if the operation is a shamble and a bad show. Better to abort it now that your tanks have got themselves stuck.'

The CO was left alone with both the bell and the cat. They say that the plan of battle is the first casualty when the first bullet is fired. Here, his whole battalion was stalled. The tanks were stuck, and the Brigade Commander had jumped quickly to sit on the fence when he received the CO's radio report about the tanks not being able to go any further. He was all for aborting the operation. The CO thought that the battalion was already inside the enemy territory. He wanted to press ahead with the attack. He had been a Tank Commander himself, and now, he was commanding a battalion of infantry. He knew instinctively what tanks and infantry could do.

'Your baby and the basket now,' said the Brigade Commander after conferring with the Divisional Headquarters. How typical of humans, he thought. Always slaved to the math of profit and loss, even when so much is at stake. Damn, damn, damn! Could he have come out with nothing better? From where do these senior jokers learn such bureaucratese? He was tempted to stand down. Why the hell should he be bothered to take the bridge if the Brigade Commander was so doubtful of the outcome? But then, he thought of the scenario from the senior officer's view. Perhaps fence-sitting was a genuine requirement at high ranks to see which side the cow of success grazed.

They were upstream from the bridge, and the idea had been to ride the tanks to the bridge and blast out the Pakistanis on it. If they kept the bridge, then their Army could come pouring into India across the Ravi river. The CO gave orders for his men to leave the tanks and come up. They were getting ready to move on and keep going to do the job. It would take time. The night was pitch dark and cold, and the fog was appearing out of nowhere. The North Indian fog, he knew, would only increase as the night wore on, forming large clouds of cottony fog where they stood. They were somewhere on the S curve of the Ravi, and the Dera Baba Nanak bridge lay somewhere invisible to the south. He knew that the Pakistanis had fortified the approaches to the bridge with machine gun nests and guns that could kill a tank at a long distance.

This was the CO's second war. He had been in the thick of things in the 1965 War's tank slugfest at Asal Uttar, where Indian tanks had created a graveyard of Pakistani tanks. The place got a nickname after the war. People curious to see knocked-out Pakistani tanks, naming it Patton Nagar.

The CO had joined the Army in 1952. He was an Armoured Corps officer. He had wanted to command his own regiment, the 3rd Cavalry. He had been in the 1965 War with his regiment, and as if by some divine inscrutable plan, he had found himself with his Tank Squadron in his own village. He knew the area only too well. It was his home and neighbourhood. The Pakistanis had thrown in hundreds of their latest American Patton tanks. His Squadron faced a regiment of the enemy's first Armoured Division rolling into Punjab, heading for Amritsar. He was the father of a one-year-old son, and his wife was expecting their second child any day now, he thought. His Squadron had been plugging at the enemy tanks, and the centurion's twenty-pounder gun was effective, very effective. The enemy was not making imaginative use of its superior strength in numbers, and the Indians were flooding the fields with canal water.

They were in the area of Kutha village, and the enemy tanks were on the horizon. He ordered his Squadron to move in. The dust rose like a desert storm was coming, and his tanks started engaging. The enemy was retaliating. All of a sudden, he felt a sledgehammer strike their tank; it was a hit. The shock flattened them against the fixtures of the tank, and he hit his head against a steel bracket. He was wearing a helmet. His head felt as if it had been grilled with a red-hot spear running right through his ears. When the wave and concussion effects had passed, he quickly tried to think, but in vain. The mind had fused into one huge, unthinking jelly mass of non-compliance. He sat rubbing his forehead, and gradually, the neurons of thought regained their old electrical pathways of logic, responsibility, and fortitude. He spoke to the driver on the tank's intercom.

'I can't make it move. I have tried everything, *sahab*. The transmission isn't working,' the tank driver informed.

There was no point sitting in a damaged tank. His crew was all right, but the tank was a goner. Thank God for the thick armour of the centurion. The tank had not blown off.

'Take out the radio set and battery,' the CO said.

Other tanks of his Squadron had seen his tank get hit. They had radioed on the regimental net that their Squadron Commander's tank was hit, and all the crew was presumed dead.

All the people of his family were stunned when they received his death telegram, including his wife, with a little baby, expecting their second child. The earth had quaked from beneath their place. There was the great void of death, the deep bottomless well in which all those who live after are left searching. The family was masked in pale sorrow. He had been the anchor of hope to everyone, the emancipator and the engine pushing everyone forward. They were left staring at the blue sky above.

Back in the dusty and sulphurous air of the battlefield, the four men disabled the tank's gun and took out the radio set and the heavy batteries to try and make it work. The spitting frontline had crossed them, and they found themselves behind the line of battle, on the side of the enemy. The CO could make out the piled-up mass of a village about a mile away. He took out his binoculars and scanned all around. The village had to be Kutha. He had come there a few times to attend marriages. They had to reach it quickly before the follow-up Army which always follows the ground won by tanks came in their wake.

They ran the mile quickly, only stopping at the village well to drink water. Then, they climbed the highest *chowbara*, a kind of top room made in the village houses of Punjab. They could see far all around.

The CO spent the day passing information on enemy movement with a map spread on his knees. The radio was really proving a great saviour. Towards the evening, the radio set batteries died, and it was no use just sitting there.

'Okay, chaps. Strip off all insignias. We will be a line party.' They had laid hands on two drums of telephone cable that had been left by some signal detachment. The four of them crossed back into Indian lines through hordes of Pakistani Army milling around them, posing as telephone line-laying signalmen of the Pakistani Army. Nobody disturbs the communication *wallas* much and they are allowed to go about their job unhindered. The ruse had worked, though they had had their close shaves. Two things had helped him in impersonation—his local Punjabi language that was no different than the Punjabi language that the Pakistani Army spoke, and his love of Urdu that made him easily pepper his talk with appropriate mannerisms of address.

He did not know that his family had been told that he was reported killed. It was after many days that the mistake was rectified, and just then, his second child came along. It was a happy time after some very bleak days for his family. In subsequent tank engagements, his Squadron had taken out about 15 enemy tanks, and he had captured a complete Pakistani Army's operational order, showing their battle plan. That enemy battleplan map is now on the heritage hall of his regiment, the 3rd Cavalry.

Five years after the 1965 War, he had been promoted to a Lieutenant Colonel's rank, but his regiment already had a CO. He was offered to command an infantry battalion, and he had gladly taken the new challenge, never being one to shy away from anything that reeked of difficulties.

The reverie of his life passed quickly. It had happened in the previous war, too; those moments of prescience when you know all the things your life has been in the flit of a second. He stared at the fog forming as if being pumped out of some giant boiler at work. There were large, grey, woolly puffs all about. He took out the compass from his belt and sat on the sand to read the map in the dim yellow light of the Army torch. He approximated and decided where they were and where the bridge could possibly be. It was clearly marked on his map, but there was no way of knowing where exactly they were.

They walked through the fog for an hour, squelching through the slush and elephant grass. They were blundering in the pitch-dark night in banks of fog. It was a hopeless task, he thought. For all they knew, they could be moving around in concentric circles. He again tried to guess the correct direction, and the Battalion again lurched and heaved, and platoons counted the heads of their men. The men walked blindly, just feeling the man in front by an outstretched hand. Some platoons had devised the trick of mountaineers and knotted the line beddings, i.e., a small length of bivouacking rope that every soldier carries, and the platoon moved following the rope. The night was dense, and the men felt visionless. There was nothing in the heavens. Not a single star, but a close jacket of cold, smoky fog that enveloped the small groups of men.

The CO looked at his watch. He didn't have much time. The daybreak was not too far off, and he didn't want to be caught here. But where could the bridge be? He had been moving on instinct alone. Had he brought his battalion correctly? If not, what could he do? The attack on the bridge may just not be possible. There was nothing but the blunt, speckless wall of darkness all around. He needed help from God; it was his last resort. He was at the end of his tether when he started praying. He was looking up at the sky with his eyes closed as he intoned the name of God, and his lips fluttered in prayer.

When he opened his eyes, there was a rent in the fog and clouds. He saw one solitary star twinkling in the vast sky. And in a flash of a second, the clouds closed in again. When he looked down from the sky, he saw the bridge in the distance, clear and unmistakable. And yet again, the fog bank closed in, and everything was dark again. He took out his compass and noted the degrees. He asked the officer standing next to him, 'Did you see the bridge?'

'No, Sir. I saw nothing,' replied the officer.

Then he turned to his radio operator, who stood next to him, with a radio set harnessed to his back and the long tape antennae swishing in the air above.

'Did you see the bridge?' he repeated the question.

'*Nahin, Sahab,*' (No, Sir) answered the radio operator.

But he was sure of what he had seen. There was no doubt in his mind, and he took the battalion unerringly to the bridge. The battalion attacked the spread-out defences of the bridge, and one of his officers daringly charged to capture an enemy machine gun which had pinned the attack of his company on the east end of the bridge. He destroyed the pill box with a grenade and pulled out the machine gun.

The next day, he was found dead with six bullets that had torn through his body. The CO, who himself was leading the charge on the enemy at the head of his men, got a bullet in the leg. He tied a tight *puttee* on his leg and rejoined his men, attacking and clearing enemy positions. The regimental medical officer had to order him to be evacuated, or he would not live through—or would, at least, lose one leg.

It is in the rarest of rare cases that one finds the CO charging the enemy-fortified positions at the head of his men personally. Only men with the DNA of a lion can do so.

Lieutenant Colonel Narinder Singh Sandhu, the CO of 10 Dogras, was awarded Mahavir Chakra, and his name remains a beacon of astonishing heroism by a CO of an infantry battalion.

His friends used to say that even in the 1965 War, he had deserved a Mahavir Chakra.

Brigadier N. S. Sandhu devoted his life to social upliftment and philanthropy after retiring from the Army. He remained Director of Youth Services of Punjab for a very long time and helped guide the youth of Punjab in a disciplined and constructive pursuit of life. He passed away in 2018, remaining active and interested in ex-servicemen affairs and matters concerning the gallantry awards forums.

Come, Fight a Gorkha!

Lacchiman Gurung was one of the 13 Gorkha soldiers who won the Victoria Cross in the Second World War. The tale of this diminutive warrior is, perhaps, unique. He was probably one of the shortest soldiers who fought in the war. His deeds stand out very tall, even in the exalted list of Victoria Cross winners, among the pillars of valour where one topples the other.

It was the winter of 1940 in a far-flung hill village in Nepal. A father told his son, 'Son, go and get me some cigarettes.'

The young man ambled off to the village shop. He met a friend who was carrying a bag slung on his back.

'Going somewhere?' asked the boy.

'I am off to *bharti* (enlistment),' replied the young man.

The two young men set off from the hills of Nepal. Generations of hill boys go to India to join the Army in their salad days. They walked over the hills, torrents, and through the forest on slippery goat tracks. Then, they hit the plains after three days. A train carried them to the town where the enrolment for the Indian Army was being done.

The *bharti* line was long. After a few hours of waiting, the boy's turn came. He felt *déjà vu*. He was 22. The *gora sahab* looked at him critically with arched eyebrows and nodded his head.

'Too short. Next.'

The young man stood on his toes and strained upwards to make up for his diminutive height. The recruiting officer smiled ruefully, 'Still too short, Johnny. Move on now.'

The young man cursed his luck. They would never enlist him. Why did he come again? If only they knew what fires burnt his heart. Had he travelled all the way to get rejected yet again? His head was hot, and blood boiled in his eyelids. He walked slowly, grimacing and cursing. The crowd of onlookers sniggered at his dejection.

'*Bona! Dekho chaar-footiya aaya bharti hone,*' (Dwarf! A four-foot dwarf has come to get enrolled) they jeered and pointed at him.

The small Gorkha kicked a stone hard that lay in his path, aiming at no one in particular. The stone flew and hit a tall, burly Pathan, who was also standing in the recruitment line. The Pathan yowled in pain and spat out brimstone and fire at the tiny Gorkha.

'*Oye khabees ka bacha*, (You wicked man) I will teach you a lesson,' screamed the frontiersman. He went to the tiny Gorkha and yanked him by the scruff of his neck violently. The Pathan looked all around to show everyone how the tiny hillman was kicking his legs in the air. He threw the Gorkha who crashed on the ground and lay in a heap. The crowd jeered, and the Pathan felt his pride restored and enlarged.

The small man got up slowly. His heart was a red coal. He charged and rammed the huge Pathan in the belly with his head with a bomb-like force. The big man fell down, and the Gorkha leapt upon him and started raining blows. He was heard shouting, 'So, you want to fight a small Gorkha. Fight me now, fight me!'

'Separate them!' yelled the recruiting officer. A few Sepoys ran forward and disentangled the duelers.

'Get him here! Get that tiny Gorkha here!' shouted the officer who had watched the event unfold in front of his eyes.

'What is your name?' asked the officer.

'*Hajur*, Lacchiman,' replied the boy.

'Write his name in the roll,' nodded the officer to his clerk.

'But, Sir, he is too short. He is not even five feet tall,' said the argumentative and officious Bengali clerk.

'Bannerji *babu*, he is tall enough as far as I am concerned. Now do as you are told,' snapped the officer with finality.

By July 1944, the Japanese Army invading Kohima and Imphal had been stopped. The Japs lost more than 60 per cent of their strength. Slim's 14th Army won hard-fought victories at Imphal and Kohima and ended the threat to India. But throwing the Japs out of Burma would take many more months.

At the end of April 1945, the 89th Brigade of the 7th Division was ordered to cross the Irrawaddy river to destroy a Japanese force which was withdrawing towards Taungdaw Valley. 4/8 Gorkha Rifles was positioned near Taungdaw village to block the route of the retreating Japanese Army.

The battalion detached two companies to lie in and block the retreating Japanese force. But, it was the Gorkhas who got encircled and cut off. On the night of 12–13 May 1945, Lacchiman was in the forward-most trench of his section, about 100 metres ahead of the rest of his platoon.

At about 1:20 ack emma[7] in the night, the Japanese assaulted them with a suicidal fury. Waves of Japanese soldiers attacked, firing and throwing hand grenades into the trenches.

7. Ack Emma refers to AM.

A grenade came and landed on Lacchiman's tin helmet. He snatched the ticking grenade and lobbed it back at the attackers before it detonated. He lobbed back a second grenade that landed in his trench in the semi-darkness of a moonlit night. Again, a grenade came and landed on the parapet of his trench. Lacchiman leaped to get hold of the grenade and tried a third 'Return to Sender'. But this time, he was not lucky. The deadly grenade went off, shattering his arm and taking off his fingers. Shrapnels cut into his right eye and his legs. The other two men in the trench also got very seriously wounded, making them *hors de combat*.

Lacchiman was wet. Blood poured out of him like a sieve —a body riddled with grenade fragments. His right eye was gone. His face was a blood mask. His right hand was mangled and gone; no fingers left. He was left with one working hand and was probably going to die very soon, he thought. He shrugged; death comes to all, he thought. What's so special if it comes to me, too?

And then, Lacchiman did what only a Gorkha can do. He pulled out his *khukhri* with his good hand and stabbed it on the parapet of his trench, and shouted at the Japanese attackers, 'None of you will make it past my *khukhri* alive!'

He picked up his bolt action Lee Enfield Mark 3 rifle, which is designed to be used by a right-handed firer, and invited the enemy, 'Come and fight a Gorkha!'

With his friends dead or dying, Lacchiman fought for hours with his one working hand, killing anyone who came near his trench. He would wait till the Japs were on top of his position. He would kill the closest Jap at point-blank range, chamber in a new round with his left hand, and then kill the Japanese soldier's battle partner. At times, he would be required to impale a Jap with his *khukhri*. This he did with divine relish.

Lacchiman killed Japanese attackers throughout the night of 12–13 May 1945 till the next morning when his company reinforcements reached his lone trench. The reinforcements heard him shouting in the haze of early morning, a solitary mad voice shouting, 'Come and fight me. Come again. I will kill you. I will kill all.'

The company held on to the critical position. Lacchiman refused to be evacuated. They counted 87 dead Japanese soldiers. Out of these, 31 had been personally killed by the tiny, badly wounded rifleman, Lacchiman Gurung.

For this stellar act of insuperable courage, Lacchiman was awarded the Victoria Cross.

He returned to his village after five years of absence without an eye and a hand. His father, Pratiman, asked him, 'Son, I had sent you to bring me cigarettes. What took you so long?'

He said, 'Father, I have got us something better than cigarettes.'

PIAT for Ganju

~

In military argot, a water truck is called bowser stainless steel, a common fork is called instrument stainless steel food four-pronged, and a khaki bedroll issued from the academy is called Wolseley Valise officers. The early anti-tank infantry weapon was called Projector Infantry Anti-Tank or PIAT. As Anton Chekhov, the great Russian short story writer, said, 'If there is a rifle hanging on the wall in a story, it must also fire.' So, our PIAT will also fire before this account is over. But first, we will take our attention to a 17-year-old boy. Yes, an Agniveer—a hopeful from Sikkim who is keen to join the Army while the Second World War rages.

The young man standing in line for recruitment was unlikely to make it. The other Gorkha aspirants eyed him with mistrust. He was tall and decidedly ungorkha in features. How could Lamas get *bharti* in the Gorkha Rifles?

The Second World War was rumbling, and the British Empire was trembling on its foundations. Days of appeasement to the Axis powers were over, and the Raj Armies were on a full-throttle recruitment drive in India. The recruitment officer nodded, and Lama moved on to the Indian clerk who was writing the recruits' particulars.

'What's your name?' the clerk asked.

'Gyamtso Shangdarpa,' the boy replied.

'What? Say again,' the clerk inquired.

'Gyamtso Shangdarpa,' the boy repeated.

The clerk scratched his head. He looked at the fair Bhutia boy. A smooth hairless face and head tonsured like a Lama—the boy was very young and raw.

'What's your age?' the clerk continued his questioning.

'Seventeen,' came the answer.

The clerk got up and went to the recruiting *sahab*.

'Never mind his age,' the *sahab* glared at him. The clerk was puzzled. What does the *sahab* see in this boy? He scratched his chin. He went back to his tin table and clipboard.

'Look here, boy. I am an educated man. Even I can't get the hang of your name. You will have trouble in the Army with this quite unpronounceable name. So, I am writing your name literally. You are bald, and you are a Lama. So, you are for the purpose of service in His Majesty's Army, Ganju Lama.'

In his battalion, Ganju was the odd boy soldier. He was young, raw, and quite untutored in his understanding of military hierarchy. His being a slightly savage Bhutia from Sikkim jungles made him the butt of jokes. He was dour and different and quite innocent.

The battalion was fighting in Burma. One morning, the senior Subedar told him to take tea for the new Company Commander. Ganju filled a mug of tea and walked to the Company Commander's field cot. The Englishman was fast asleep. Ganju said loudly, 'Uth!' (Get up!) The Englishman remained sleeping. Ganju again shouted, 'Uth!'

The Company Commander was dead asleep. The Subedar and his chums watched the unfolding spectacle with a keen expectation of free entertainment. In fact, they had hatched this plan to get Ganju Lama on the wrong side of the Company Commander. The boy was young, and he had not yet learnt etiquettes and dignified subservience of the military order. And he was a Bhutia among Gorkhas.

Ganju again shouted, '*Uth! Chai pee!*' (Get up! Have tea!)

The officer kept sleeping. A frustrated Ganju kicked the camp cot hard and woke up the officer. In doing so, hot tea splashed from his mug and fell on the officer. The latter got up and rubbed his eyes. He took the tea mug from Ganju and said, 'Thank you, that will be all.'

That morning, Subedar Gumm Bahadur, the senior Subedar, was walking with the Company Commander.

'*Sahab*, that clumsy new boy is not fit to be your Batman. He came and told me that he kicked your charpoy and spilt tea on you. If *sahab* affirms, I will give him ten days' *pitthu* and extra guard duties.'

'Whatever for? I quite liked the boy, Subedar *sahab*. He is bold and fearless and takes initiative. Let him be.'

Subedar *sahab* scratched his head. The English *sahabs* had strange minds. One could never guess what they are thinking. Anyhow, he had other ways to sort out that arseling. The company had received a heavy anti-tank weapon called PIAT. He schemed and got Ganju to carry a PIAT along with his rifle. This amused the senior JCO.

Soon thereafter, one day, their company deployed in Ningthoukhong faced a Japanese tank attack. The three Japanese tanks advanced with their machine guns, mowing everything in front of them. The main guns of the tanks blazed and started creating havoc. The company would soon be overrun and cease to exist. Ganju got hit in two places—his right leg and left hand. His wrist broke. With his flesh still burning, he dashed forward with his PIAT within 30 yards and knocked out the tanks that threatened to decimate his company. The tank crews bailed out. Ganju closed in, grievously injured himself, but sent them all to Valhalla with grenades. For this magnificent episode of bravery, the obnoxious 19-year-old boy was awarded the Victoria Cross.

Later on, Ganju Lama also won a Military Medal at Tiddim Road for exceptional courage. By now, his name was a legend.

Once, I happened to visit Gangtok Bazaar after our *paltan* completed the annual field firing in Sikkim. An ex-soldier started chatting with me in the bazaar. He pointed out a door where a few men were sitting in the sun, counting prayer beads.

'Victoria, Victoria,' he said and pointed at the group of men.

I didn't quite understand him. But I walked with him to the men. He kept saying 'Victoria' and gesticulating towards an oldish man. A quiet man sat silently amidst the group, flicking prayer beads. It was Subedar Major, Honorary Captain Ganju Lama, VC, MM of the 1/7th Gorkha Rifles, and later 11 GR. He was appointed honorary ADC to the President of India for life.

The Giant of Palda and the Banzai Charges

Beware of going there because of running death.

—A Japanese soldier to another soldier going in for a Banzai charge on the Indian gun position of Havildar Umrao Singh, and his eight men.

Few people ever came out alive facing repeated Banzai charges and lived to tell the tale. Captain Umrao Singh's Victoria Cross was awarded based on the testimony of Japanese prisoners during the after-battle interrogations.

There is no greater honour for a soldier than being praised by your enemy.

Many years later, a lad who had come to our village boasted, 'There is a Victoria in our village.'

The lad had come to get his buffalo crossed with our village's handsome and gigantic bison. It would be a long affair of animal amour to locate the bison and then lure him to the spiral-horned buffalo.

I failed to make a head or tail when he said this. I thought he might be speaking of some Christian woman. Puzzlingly, Western names sometimes find their way into folk talk in our parts of Haryana. One day, I heard someone tell me that his grandfather had been to *Kunstuntuniya* when he was in the Army. It took me years to realise, despite a lot of head-scratching, that he had probably meant Constantinople, today's Istanbul.

Another time, I ran into some Ahirs of our area. They said that the real *sher* (tiger) lived in their village, Palda, which was about two miles from my village. The village people, simple-minded folks, are given to humour built around exaggeration, leg-pulling and jeering. I was a young officer in the Army. I came on leave and got to hear the talk of the people, besides the usual ugly badgering one has to face:

'*Mhaarey chhorey ne bharti karaa de. Tu kissa afsar sae? Afsar tayy paddey rookh Ney bharti karaa de.*' (Get my son recruited. What kind of officer are you? An officer can get a fallen tree stump recruited if he wishes.)

One day, I was amazed to hear a talk in the village. An old man said that the village was once the capital of Haryana, and we had a king who belonged to a very far-off country called 'Ahirland'. Later on, when the reading bug caught me, and I started blitzing well-stocked Army libraries, I discovered that, indeed, our village had an astonishing link to the past. George Thomas, the Raja of Haryana, a sailor from Tipperary in Ireland, indeed, had made Jahazgarh his capital in 1798. Georgegarh had been rounded off to the nearest approximate Haryanvi sound and called Jahazgarh. And Ireland had conveniently approximated to match Ahirland or Heerland.

Much of today's Haryana was denominated 'crown land' of the sultans and kings of Delhi. The revenue directly went to the king's chauffeurs, and he administered these lands directly and not through any vassals. Ferozeshah Tughlak, whose mother was a native Haryanvi woman, was the person who planned to irrigate the desert tracts of old Haryana by having canals dug that brought Yamuna water right up to his city called Hissar Feroza, today's Hissar. There canals were called *ulughkhani* and *rajabwaah* canals. To this day, the smaller government water channels are called rajbhaayas. The Turks and the Mughals settled a lot of people of Pathan stock in Haryana. A majority of Haryanvi villages have Islamic names.

But in my initial years of service, I had wondered how our twin hamlets of Jahazgarh Majra could be the capital of a kingdom. It was the land of idle fellows and idle talk over the gurgle of hookahs.

One wrote a blue inland letter costing ten paise home to inform the folks about one's approximate dates of reaching the village. One would hitch rides in tongas and camel carts, and invariably, it would be dark before one reached home.

'Can't you ever come home in the daytime like decent folk? You always reach home in darkness,' chided my mother. It was very difficult to explain to folks who had never gone beyond an arc of ten miles how vast the distances of Hindustan were.

When I'd come on leave, the father would be waiting to decree. 'You may be an officer in your *paltan*, but here you are a farmer's son.' And he would list out the back-breaking farm chores that had to be taken care of. Weed the fields; bring a *bharota* on your head; take the buffaloes grazing; come home and weave hempen ropes. That was the existential ethic of my family, enforced by the leather-faced patriarch of many blistering summers. Once back in the village, you forgot pants and shirts and slipped quietly into a whitish kurta-pyjama, and merged into the surroundings.

Village houses were not built to any plan of architecture. They were square boxes of mud bricks and beamed roofs covered with a matting of sticks over which a six-inch layer of *chikni mitti* or clay was spread. In the summer, loos galloped through and through, and the earth burned, and in winters, thick frost carpeted everything. Retired soldiers came with few possessions, the prized things being the *garm shirt*, shirt Angola, the jersey, but the *fauji kaamba* (blanket barrack) was the most sought-after article.

Military medals of older forebears, ribbons holed by silverfish and *kisaari* lay at the bottom of wooden boxes. The hard-pressed womenfolk would give them to babies for amusement. The babies, seeing some new gaudy ribbon and shiny metal, would stop bawling for a while. They would take the silver Queen Victoria head in their mouth and rub tender gums on sweet metal, and try to eat metal, and in excess of heat, tire out and sleep.

When the Partition took place, cruelly dislocated people who had been living in Punjab for centuries started coming to villages, ever willing to trade grain for utensils, cloth, and other things.

The practical but dunderheaded Haryanvi women brought out medals embossed with images of kings and queens and exchanged them for *paraats* and *patilaas*. To their sense of economy of running a household, it made sense to give away an Indian Order of Merit Medal for a small pan or a *tawa*.

One day, I thought I would go and see who the Victoria in the neighbouring village was rather than get myself knackered by incessant labour at my father's farm as usual. I walked the two miles, and reached Palda. I asked someone where I could see the Victoria. The person pointed an arm, indicating onwards. So, after obtaining many directions and misdirections and perambulating in and out of lanes, I finally found myself walking towards the village pond. The silver water was broken by humps of black cattle swimming in it. In the farther reaches of the pond, water hens and ducks swam in the weeds, diving and coming up. It was the month of June, and the pond water had receded, revealing a wide foreshore of clay and fine gravel. The sun was throwing tridents of heat, and the hot winds raced breathlessly, roasting everything in their path. The cheery sounds of nature enjoying the Indian scorch were all around—the wind shingling through *sheesham* pods, the chirruk-chirruk of birds. A crested kingfisher hovered ten metres above the lapping waves on its tail. It stood still in the air, and then, like a thunderbolt, it pulled its wings into its sides and struck into the water. Soon, it was out with a small fish and flew away.

A man sat on the ground, patiently looking at the buffaloes. So this was the Victoria, whose legend rang in the *gaon-guhaand* (local area).

I walked up to him and said, 'Ram-Ram *sahab*.' He sat under the dappled shadow of a *sheesham* tree. The wind sang among the pale brown pods, hanging in bunches like women's ornaments. The honey bees were at work, buzzing like dull cellos, flirting among the pale-yellow flowers of the tree. Black *makodaas* (big ants) ran up and down the crevices of the tree barks, running their own busy errands.

When I introduced myself as an officer of the artillery, the man who had been supervising the swimming buffaloes stood up and said, 'Ram-Ram *sahab*, Ram-Ram *sahab*.' His pleasure at meeting me showed all over his beaming face. He was a mountain of a man, towering above six feet by many inches. I stood facing a pillar of our history. A great, great Indian. It was because of the feats of men like him that the world sat up and took note of Indians when the world groaned under Axis tyranny and India faced a modern invasion from the Japanese Empire. Mahatma Gandhi had said, reading of Umrao Singh's feats in the newspapers, 'The heroism and bravery of the sons of India. The world is watching, and they are helping establish freedom around the world for others. But do not yet have freedom themselves.'

This was the totally unpretentious, artifice-less Haryanvi farmer for whom British Deputy Prime Minister Michael Heseltine had stopped his car in London and said, 'How can I cross the road when a Victoria Cross is walking across the road?'

He had walked up to Captain Umrao Singh and saluted him and said, 'Sir, thank you for your services. Without India's support, Britain would never have emerged victorious in the World Wars.'

The story of Umrao Singh VC will always be heralded as one of the greatest acts of heroism and valour. He has a special place on the wall of the Royal Artillery in London where the names of VCs are inscribed.

The 30th Mountain Regiment of the Royal Artillery had spent the monsoon season of 1944 with the 25th Indian Division around Maungdaw Bauthidong area. By the end of October, the 32nd and 33rd batteries were transferred to the 81st West African Division. After three weeks of marching, they reached their new operational area in the Kaladan Valley on 21 November 1944. Although the division was only 60 miles from the coast, it was shut off by a range of 2,000-foot mountains and a barrier of solid bamboo forests. They hacked, cleared and levelled several airstrips for supply by Dakotas of transport command and to remain in contact with the rest of the 15 Corps. The east-most flank of the division was shelled constantly by the Japanese 28th Army.

On 15 December 1944, Havildar Umrao Singh was in charge of a 3.7-inch Howitzer position when he found himself at the receiving end of a Japanese offensive. After a long artillery and mortar shelling, the Japanese thought that everything in front of them was obliterated. About 400 Japanese charged forward as a human wave shouting, 'Banzai, Banzai.'

By December 1944, the Japanese government had announced the last protocol, unofficially named Ichioku

Gyokusai, meaning 100 million shattered jewels, implying the will to sacrifice the entire Japanese population of 100 million to achieve victory.

The Banzai charge is considered to be one of the methods of Gyokusai, i.e., shattered jewel or honourable suicide. The Japanese soldiers believed, 'A true and honourable man would rather be a shattered jewel than an intact tile or brick.' It was part of the Bushido code of the Japanese to be ideologically obedient to the emperor.

Umrao Singh stood facing the elite troops of Japan's empire. The Japanese had a personal code—fighting a war for their country was purifying and, death, in the war, was a soldier's duty.

Umrao Singh and his men fired for up to six hours in the battle, pulling off one of the greatest defences of an exposed position. The dead were piling up around them. They had repelled the first Banzai of the enemy. The next day, the Japanese again came shouting, 'Banzai-Banzai'.

By now, they realised that they were out of ammunition. They had fired the last round of the Howitzer. All that they had were a few magazines of the Bren gun (light machine gun) left. On the 16th morning came the definitive Banzai charge. Only Umrao Singh and two other men were left by now. Six men of his gun section had died in the fights. When nothing was left, and the Japanese closed in to finish off the last remnants after having lobbed grenades at the Indian position, a badly wounded man picked up a gun bearer, a kind of iron rod used to shift the gun, and closed in with the Banzais who closed in to bayonet him and take his head off. Even the attacking Japanese had run out of ammunition by now.

Nobody saw this battle; gallants stand against overwhelming odds. After the battle was over, and the British and Indian forces reached the plateau, they found Umrao Singh and two others wounded but alive. Umrao Singh had been wounded so severely that they could not even tell whether he was Japanese or Indian. But around Umrao Singh were ten dead Japanese who had been bludgeoned to death. He still held the gun spike in his hands when he was discovered lying among the dead Japanese.

The astonished British officer looked at the terrain and the wounded. How in the name of hell could anyone have survived the fury of the Japanese attack was beyond his reckoning. They had heard the fighting, and it had taken them two days to reach the area with reinforcements.

An unconscious Umrao Singh was evacuated and sent to the hospital, where he did eventually recover from his wounds. The British reinforcing unit managed to collect a few surviving wounded Japanese prisoners. During the post-battle interrogations, it came out that the Japanese had mentioned this one giant Indian soldier who seemed to be everywhere at any given time, stalling their attack. One of the Japanese soldiers had said to his comrade, pointing at Umrao Singh's position, 'Beware of going there because of running death.'

Umrao Singh's two surviving mates also gave their after-action report.

Umrao Singh had been wounded by grenades twice during the first assault. When the intelligence reports reached General Slim, the Army Commander, and he read of Umrao Singh's glorious tenacity and actions and the feedback of the Japanese prisoners, he ordered the CO of Umrao Singh's unit to forward the man's name for awarding the Victoria Cross.

The smiling giant of Palda used to be a regular and honoured national hero along with other Param Vir Chakra and Victoria Cross awardees at Republic Day parades in Delhi. He died on his very birthday, 21 November, in 2005—India's last Victoria Cross winner.

Out of the 21 Victoria Crosses awarded to soldiers of undivided India in the Second World War, the tiny state that forms today's Haryana has five Victoria Cross winners. The total Indian Army strength was 2.5 million strong. One can imagine how high and rare the valour that got the Victoria Cross was!

Marriage Ring Inside a White Egg

Shimla was the cool seat of the British Raj in blue hills. I spent four feral childhood years in the deodar valleys of Shimla.

A faded childhood memory comes like a flying petrel. A magic show at the big General's house for all kids of Shimla station on 15 August 1983 ignites a primus stove of recollections.

We used to live in a four-roomed cottage called NX 8, just adjacent to Charing Cross at Jutogh Cantt, a satellite of Shimla, a few miles away. When the rhesus monkeys ran down the wooded slope, they exploded on our cottage's tin roof like a hail storm. I would rush out with my catapult and a bag of cement musket balls and embattle with the monkeys. A Jeep's tube rubber made the best catapults, and I made my own ammunition with cement and sand. Nothing great; all boys, if left feral by their parents, do such things. The cottage was in a valley, and the sun only touched it for a few hours every day. It had no privacy. The road to Shimla passed right above it, and every groaning engine's whines echoed against the cottage walls. On the other side was a modern carton box housing complex. The silent green-roofed church with a steeple overlooked our house.

Sometimes, I trespassed through my father's unfathomable Military History books that covered a shelf. I realised that very violent events had happened on Earth. Our land had been ruled by clever and more organised people—alien people. The evidence was everywhere. The 50-metre tall radio mast that transmitted radio signals straight to London stood in Jutogh, kissing the clouds.

One day, many three-tonne trucks lined up at Charing Cross right in front of our cottage gate. They were full of women and children of the cantonment. The trucks started, and we went to Shimla via Mall Road, where no vehicles were normally allowed to ply. We got down and walked up the road into the compound of a large bungalow. Rows of *shamianas* were put around a raised dais, and we kids were told to sit. We sat on the ground, and soon, a senior officer in a dark green coat came and sat on a sofa. A magician appeared on the stage and started performing. He took out a white pigeon from an empty hat with the flourish of his stick upon the hat. The white bird flailed its pinions and soared, free and happy.

The magician had a pot, which he called the water of India. Every few minutes, he would upturn it, and this vessel always refilled itself. Then, he asked a married woman to come to the stage. After a while, a woman walked up to the stage. The magician took her marriage ring and made it disappear. The woman cried out, 'Give my ring back!'

The magician gave the woman a white egg. The woman said, 'My ring cost me a lot of money. I won't be fobbed off by a 25 *naya paisa* egg in return.'

The magician asked her to break the egg in a pan. The lady took a spoon and cracked the egg. And lo and behold, her gold ring was there inside the cracked egg!

I was very young then, but memory of the egg trick has remained fresh in my mind as being a portent of things which exist but are not seen—remain cleverly hidden.

The officers' mess across Charing Cross used to get a newspaper, which used to be on a reading stand in the entrance. A newspaper brought the whole world within arm's reach. The world was huge and exotic, and you could only see it in a newspaper. Two boys from Jutogh cantonment got selected for NDA. One was my father's unit's JCO, Subedar A's son. Subedar A was a very dapper JCO. I have never seen a man wearing more gleaming black shoes than him. He wore black Oxford shoes with a darned patch stuck on them. The gleam of the highly polished shoes gave them dignity. I felt that a thing that is worth keeping is worth a repair. The other boy was Major C's son. He strolled down the church slope, hand-in-hand with his sister. They were smart kids and inseparable. I used to think what Didi would feel once her inseparable appendage brother went away. The cantonment whispered the fact of these two boys heading for NDA. It seemed like the trees also knew their names and sang the fact. I used to feel that when the wind blew, the deodars announced the news of their selection in NDA.

For many days, I replayed in my mind the delightful tricks of the magician in the Army Commander's house. I remembered the sparse-haired, graceful and kindly figure of the General in his green double-breasted coat. Then, I heard whispers that the General who gave us kids the magic show would be going to Delhi to assume charge of the whole Indian Army.

I learnt that the General had gone to Delhi just from overhearing the grown-ups talk. Though absolutely indifferent to all subjects, I had a habit of reading. The mess at Charing

Cross had the day's newspaper (*Times of India*) displayed on a rack in the foyer. I used to go to the mess to collect milk in a *dollu*. My father deputed me to do minor household chores. He insisted that I share the weight of running a family unit. I never minded work. I only minded it when he showed me angry eyes after reading my school report card. Soon, a few stinging slaps would assert the right to education for me. Then, I used to think that I was free till the next report card. When my marks would come, I would be aware that their derisory value would invite another avalanche of beatings. I was fond of pens and calligraphy. I picked up my father's grey Parker and signed his signature. Having averted a catastrophe for some time, I would again smell freedom and joy.

One day, I stopped and flipped the pages of the newspaper in the mess. I was utterly dismayed as I read the headlines. It said that our General of the magic show was not going to head the Army. Someone else had been chosen in his stead. I felt very deflated. It was unfair. The much-looked-forward-to magic show in Delhi rose in vapours and melted.

It is well known that Lieutenant General S. K. Sinha is the only chief designate who put up his papers when the government of the day superseded him in a Machiavellian sleight. General Sinha was one of the only three Indian officers in the Army Headquarters' Military Operations Directorate on the eve of India's independence. The other two Indians were Sam Manekshaw and Yahya Khan. Even the clerks of this super-secret directorate were Englishmen in 1947.

I have read a few times that on the eve of Partition, Lieutenant General Nathu Singh had voiced doubts about continuing with a British General as the head of our Army. He had questioned Prime Minister Nehru's wisdom in doing so. An exasperated Nehru had replied, 'Indians have no experience of heading the Army.'

Then, Thakur Nathu Singh is purported to have replied, 'Well, Indians have never headed the government either before, why not invite an Englishman to become India's Prime Minister?'

During the crucial time from 15 August 1947 to 31 December 1947, General Rob Lockhart was the Chief of the Indian Army. Lockhart had spent the entire Second World War in various appointments at Army HQ in New Delhi. On the eve of independence, he was the General Officer Commanding (GOC), Southern Command. Lockhart had joined the 51st Sikh Regiment as a Second Lieutenant in March 1914 and served through the First World War in Egypt, Aden, and Mesopotamia.

His compatriot, the Pakistan Army Chief, was the legendary soldier of repute, master tactician, and widely-experienced General, Sir Frank Messervy KCSI, KBE, CB, DSO, and BAR. Messervy had been handpicked for the last act of the great game by the departing British. The stage was closing for the British Empire—the curtain was falling, but a final *coup de grace* remained. Messervy was also an old Indian Army hand, having joined the 9th Hodsons Horse upon commissioning in France during the First World War.

Messervy was an early prophet of unorthodox tenets of warfare. At the outbreak of the Second World War, he was sent with the 5th Indian Division to Sudan as its GSO. Facing the Italians, he was appointed to raise the 'Gazelle Force'—a mobile recce and strike force for commando operations of an expanded battalion size. Later on, in the North African campaign, he was the only British Indian Army officer to command a British Division during WWII.

Messervy was an unorthodox General. He was known as 'The Bearded Man' because he tended not to shave in battle. His Divisional Headquarters was overrun by Rommel's forces at the start of the Battle of Gazala. The divisional General Officer

Commanding, General Messervy, was captured by German troops. But removing all insignia of rank, he managed to bluff the Germans into believing that he was just an ordinary Batman. Later on, he escaped the clutch of the Germans with members of his staff and rejoined his division. Closer home, Messervy's role in the battles of Imphal and Kohima is more widely known to our officer class. What is not known is his role in Pakistan's (shall we say a fading British Empire's) role to forcibly acquire Kashmir, an unaffiliated princely state, for the Western Allied powers.

Jinnah, who was a quisling of the Britishers, had assured the Empire that Pakistan would always be on their side for granting them a pure Muslim homeland. While all Congress leaders had been thrown in jail from 1942 to 1945 following the Quit India Movement, Mr Jinnah had been allowed to have a free run to incubate the egg of a separate Muslim homeland all over India, and he didn't sit idle. He made the most of the opportunity, spreading poison and hatred in the minds of Indians and exhibiting and hawking his pet obsession naked, the two-nation theory.

By July 1947, all the areas of North-West Frontier Provinces and Baluchistan Frontier had been emptied of all Hindu and Sikh personnel of the Indian Army. Tribesmen were being recruited. Same tribesmen who would be channelised into the invasion of Kashmir. This decision was taken in a conference presided over by General Auchinleck. But as fate had decreed, on the eve of Partition, an Indian Sikh Major, Onkar Singh Kalkat, found himself stuck in Bannu on the wrong side of the border. Kalkat was the Brigade Major of the Bannu Frontier Force Brigade. On 20 August, the usual Army *daak* bag (postal bag) arrived at the HQ, and he signed for it. He sifted through the brown envelopes. All of them were the usual *daak* until his eyes fell on a thick envelope sealed with red wax and marked 'Top Secret' and addressed to Brigadier C. P. Murray. When he opened the letter, there was a DO letter signed by General Messervy, The Bearded Man of old, accompanied by a detailed operational plan for the invasion and capture of Kashmir. The letter had come from Rawalpindi Army Headquarters.

Kalkat's Brigade Commander was visiting the Mirali outpost, 41 km away from Bannu. Kalkat informed the Brigadier on the radio about receiving the plan of Operation Gulmarg. The Brigadier told him to keep his mouth shut because if anybody came to know that he knew the Gulmarg operational plan, he would not leave Pakistan alive. Major Kalkat copied the plan. A junior Muslim officer at the Brigade HQ got suspicious, and the next morning, Kalkat was arrested by the Lieutenant, who was accompanied by an Englishman. The Englishman quipped to Kalkat, 'You just poked your nose into something too big.'

Kalkat very audaciously and resourcefully managed to escape and reach Delhi with his information, risking his life and limb for his country. Here, a Brigadier and the Colonel laughed at Kalkat's information. They called it a cock and bull tale concocted under duress of separation from family, Partition, and overzealous patriotism. Like good bureaucrats, they told the Defence Minister Sardar Baldev Singh about it. The Defence Minister asked the Military Intelligence section for their opinion. The MI was totally staffed by the British. They promptly said it was a cock and bull tale. The Brigadier even called his friends on the military hotline at Pakistan Army HQ, who he said had laughed aloud at the suggestion and promised everlasting brotherhood between India and Pakistan.

Operation Gulmarg was personally directed by Messervy from his house in Rawalpindi. Once, in between, he went to the UK (we can guess he went for a special briefing and orders too precious to be communicated via radio or post), and on his way back, he slipped in via New Delhi. Operation Gulmarg had not yet started. Mountbatten had made him swear that he

(Messervy) had not been asked for, nor had he provided any help to the tribesmen. Within a week, he was found providing arms, ammunition, RAF lorries, and everything else from Rawalpindi arsenal to the Pathan *lashkars*. He was in cahoots with George Cunningham, who was the Governor of NWFP (North-West Frontier Province). He complained to Governor Cunningham, 'Mountbatten has gone over to the side of the Hindus.'

Both Messervy, as Pakistan Army Chief, and his Deputy Chief, General Douglas Gracey, supervised and directed, on a day-to-day basis, the invasion of Kashmir from the mansion in Rawalpindi. How very British, they usually had a habit of separate houses for each separate operation/department to work from. Regular Pakistan Army officers, JCOs and NCOs were loaned out to command the *lashkars* and shown on records as being absent. Messervy issued a statement on 12 November 1947, denying that any, 'serving Pakistani Army officers are directing operations in Kashmir.' Messervy relieved his post as Pakitan Army Chief on 15 February 1948 after duly securing strategic areas of Jammu and Kashmir, as he had been directed to do by the British government.

Two other Englishmen were superbly playing their supporting role of Judas in the big game on the Kashmiri Raja's side. His Inspector General of Police, Richard Powell, and his Chief of State Forces' Brigadier Henry Lawrence Scot, CBI, DSO, BAR, MC. This helpful gentleman had scattered the 8 infantry battalions of J&K State Army all over the borders from Ladakh to Kathua. He was hand in glove with Cunningham, the Governor of NWFP, who had been recruiting tribals since Auchinleck's conference in the summer of 1946.

The only J&K state forces battalion on the gateway of Kashmir Valley was at Domel and Muzzafarabad, commanded by Lieutenant Colonel Narain Singh. His battalion had 40 per cent Muslim troops. He ignored warnings to disarm his Muslim companies. He said they were his most trusted comrades, who had fought with distinction in Burma with him. These Muslim troops were in the know of the plans of Operation Gulmarg, and when the hour struck, they very cordially slit the throats of their sleeping Hindu comrades in one mass tide of treachery. They didn't spare their trusting but gullible CO, Lieutenant Colonel Narain Singh, either. The highway to the Valley was now open.

The other stalwart liegeman of George the Sixth left Indian shores on 1 December 1947, Field Marshal Claude Auchinleck of the Punjab Regiment. The nemesis of Rommel, not once, but twice. The finest General on the British side, as per Alanbrooke, the CIGS, 'He had the knack for choosing bad subordinates.'[8]

In the end, the Englishmen were superbly loyal to their government and its orders and, like good generals, never tired of planning invasions, operations, deception, and capturing places. Truth is always protected by a bodyguard of lies.

Nobody can see a marriage ring inside a white egg.

---

8. Rommel was the legendary Desert Fox, the Commander of the Afrika Corps.The greatest General of mechanised warfare, who was adversary of Claude Auchinleck in North Afrika in WWII. Alanbrooke was the Chief of Imperial General Staff, who was the main advisor of Winston Churchill, Britain's wartime PM. Auchinleck, after North African campaign, was appointed Commander-in-Chief India, when General Wavell was appointed Viceroy before Mountbatten came in. Wavell came after Linlithgow.

The Old Breed

~

I have known only one soldier intimately in my life. He was impervious to heat, cold, dust, discomfort, and all the wall hooks on which we hang the joys and sorrows of life. His only vice was reading and acquisition of knowledge. His spartan and frugal ways would scare even boneless beggars. He found it impossible to spend money. He would go with a bottle of military rum to Daryaganj footpath booksellers in Delhi and return with a pile of hardbound books by reputed international book publishers. He would then write on the front page of the books, 'Purchased by me for 1/6th bottle of rum'. Then, he would diligently sign and date the entry. I always thought he was cracked and heavily eccentric in the head. The only thing he feared was poverty.

He loved his mother devotedly. He never saw his father, who died when he was a baby. A bullock cart wheel had run over the toes of his father. The crushed foot had got septicemia, resulting in his death. In his life, my friend hardly mentioned his father. But he did not say any bad things about him. He did say, at times, that his father was feckless and lazy and had done nothing noticeable in his life. He came like mud and slipped away like sand from the hand of life. His maker was his mother and mother alone.

Once, I read his notebooks. Green plastic-covered notebooks whose paper had yellowed and the fountain pen words took me into his life when he was a young man. He was a student and a farmer. He had written a favourite declaration, which even I had heard him utter on rare occasions of nostalgia, 'I love my mother more than anyone in this world. But my work is even dearer to me than my mother.'

It fell upon me to sort out his stuff after he died. In impecunious families like mine, one passes a lifetime making a shield wall against dense clouds of poverty. One doesn't know one's parents even after living for many years in their shadow.

We had an old medieval house in our village. Well, not our original village but our second village, to which our family migrated. The house that we got allotted belonged to a Muslim Ranghar *zamindar*.

His college diaries, that I read after his death, were full of expenditure summaries. If he drank tea in the college canteen, he wrote the expenditure in his diary and then wrote, 'Was the tea necessary? Couldn't I do without tea?' He had also written the names of people whom he could approach for money. He had analysed and listed people from whom he could flannel money to meet his college expenditure. He never had money to pay the fees or buy clothes. He had written that he felt helpless in front of the disabling poverty that he was facing. He was an outstanding academic scholar, standing first in the college for all three years. He spoke English better than anyone I have met. His prize books, mostly works of authors like Jane Austen and Thomas Hardy, are my most cherished possessions today.

In 1969, after graduating from Jat College in Rohtak, he was selected for the Short Service Ninth course at Officers Training School, Madras. He used to tell me how he just managed to reach in time for the SSB at Meerut.

One late evening, he arrived after appearing for teachers' selection exams at Rewari. Our Gochhi was a remote village. Grandma gave him a telegram as soon as he reached home.

'Here, this wire (*taar*) came for you while you were away,' she said.

It was a telegram informing him that he was to present himself for the Services Selection Board interview at 0800 hours at Meerut the very next morning. He just had one worn-out threadbare trouser and a much-frayed shirt, and he was already wearing them. He went out to borrow clothes from his friends and got a shirt, pants, and shoes on loan. He borrowed someone's bicycle and started pedalling towards Sonepat, about 50 miles away. Beyond Sonepat flowed the Yamuna, and the lights of Baghpat twinkled beyond. On the Yamuna bridge, the back-sore cyclist met a truck loaded with raw bananas grinding to Meerut on the broken road. Luck had been kind to him. He left his bicycle at a puncture shop. The driver said, 'You can ride on the cab top if you like.' He climbed up only to be shown teeth by the driver's pet monkey on the roof of the truck's cabin. The monkey didn't take the intrusion in a brotherly manner. He was hungry. He ate a couple of raw bananas and slept on a bed of banana leaves. The monkey accepted his presence as a fact of life. The driver thankfully dropped him at the cantonment. And that's how he made it for his SSB with a sore bottom, redder than a monkey's from all the cycling.

I was just 12 years old when he arrived with an old Army mare in a tempo truck. He said, 'You will feed this horse, water it, and look after it. You can also learn horse riding on it.'

Officers all around were contemplating buying the new Maruti 800 car that cost ₹45,000. He had a snoring old Lambretta scooter and a 24-inch black Atlas bicycle. And he had added an old sixteen-hand mare to our locomotion options. It was an auction horse from the Army stud farm at Babugarh near Ghaziabad.

The bay mare stood in the garage with its head hanging down. I filled a tin bucket with water and kept it in front of her.

My friend said, 'Go to the village lumberdar and get some *bhoosee* (wheat stalk chaff).' My feet barely reached the bicycle's pedals. I rode it, pushing the pedals with my toes on the upper half trajectory. The lumberdar kept a cattle feed shop in Challera village. He looked up at me sceptically, 'Your father has got a horse?'

'Yes,' I replied.

'And you want *bhoosee* for it?' asked the lumberdar.

'Yes, that's what he said,' I gave the lumberdar the note written by my father in his elegant fountain pen handwriting. My father was fond of good pens and had a pen pot full of Sheaffers and Parkers.

The lumberdar called out one of his sons, 'Take this boy and fill his sack with *bhoosee*.' He helped me hoist the bloated sack on the carrier and then pull the securing cycle tube over the seat.

It was impossible to ride the high bicycle with the huge sack. I walked with the bicycle through the black slush of the village streets of 1980s India. The gleaming steel rim of the tyres squelched through a stinking slurry of village streets, which were also drains. I balanced the sack with one hand and the handlebar with the other. A steel *dollu* of *chaach* (buttermilk) also hung on the handlebar that the lumberdar had insisted on being taken to his friend. As I was pushing the bicycle, a strange thing flew and smarmed my face. I froze and tried to take off the gelatin-like creature from my face. Well, in a moment, the bat flew off. No wonder they call bats blind. The foolish creature came and spread itself on my face. My heart shivered, but I retained my grip on the sack and the handlebar and soldiered on and reached home.

We learnt later that horses eat dry grass, neither paddy hay nor *bhoosee*. We were both ignorant. A few days later, my friend took out an old Sherman tank helmet from his tin trunk, got an old saddle and bit from some *tongawalla*.

'Now you must start riding,' he said to me.

He took me to the open ground where the Noida Sector 37 golf course stands today. The land had been acquired by the government from the farmers of Challera village. There was an old war memorial pillar commemorating the Anglo-Maratha wars there. I got the horse; it was a docile one. It started a swinging canter. I had never before sat on anything except a few small white donkeys in my village. My riding skills were non-existent, but pride kept me sticking on the saddle. The horse suddenly came to a halt in front of a grassy thicket. I saw my father in the distance, standing and observing me. I wanted to make a good impression on him. I had heard him say that many of our forebears had been in cavalry and were crack horsemen in their times. I heeled the lugubrious mare; it skittered on the grass bank and suddenly slid down hindwards into the ground. I had not seen it, but there was a wide unused well covered with tall grass. We were both falling into it. I thought that was the end, but somehow, the noble mare started kicking with her hind legs, and I was thrown just on the edge of the well. I lay on the ground, watching her as she hung half inside the well. I got up, held her reins, and started pulling her and exhorting her to make more effort. I was a 40-kilo boy, and she was a 500-kilo horse. Finally, she did pull herself out of the well. I held her reins and started walking. My father had started walking towards us.

'What's the matter? Why aren't you in the saddle?' he asked in a hard voice.

'We fell in a well,' I answered.

'Which well? Show me,' he insisted.

I walked ahead and pointed to the well and the circle of black water deep down.

He glared at me and said, 'Are you an idiot? Couldn't you see the well? Be more careful in the future. Now get on the horse and start riding.'

The Cup Bearers

~

'Get up my sweetest, it is dawn. Gently, gently sip the wine and twang the harp,' suggests Omar Khayyam in *Rubaiyat*.

I was a young Lieutenant posted in Meerut. After a hard day's work, I entered the oak-panelled bar of the Wheelers Club. Once you cross the byzantinian pillars of the club, you enter the splendour of a bygone age. The old world's tide is washing into the new. Even the paintings and silver plaques sigh and whisper mysteries from the walls.

A very tall, stooped old bartender stood behind the bar counter. 'One Old Monk, please,' I said.

The old man looked at me as if woken up from a private reverie. He had a kindly face.

'Sir, you don't drink whisky?' he asked me in a clipped English accent. I was not even 25 and unfamiliar with drinks and the offerings of Bacchus.

'Very well, give me a whisky then,' I said to placate the affronted dignity of this ancient priest of thc temple of Bacchus.

'Peter Scott, *sahab*?' he asked.

'Yes, please,' I said in my most dulcet tone.

His hands quivered as he poured the golden liquid into the hourglass peg measure.

'Is it your first visit to this club, Sir?' he asked.

'Indeed, it is,' I ventured.

'My good Sir, rum is only to be drunk by officers during the war,' claimed the man.

'And why so?' I asked.

'Because it is a drink of rage and passion,' said Ramchandra, the head barman of Wheelers Club.

A few years later, I went to do the Junior Command course at Mhow. On the last day of the course, I and a friend of mine went to the Mhow Officers Club. I took out the money and kept it on the bar counter. The barman was a very spruce-looking man of medium height. He was fair-complexioned and had a darkish rub mark on his forehead that accrues from regularly rubbing one's head on the floors of places of worship. That evening, we left the club late, and the next day, we boarded trains to return to our units.

Life continued, and after ten years, I again found myself in Mhow to do the Senior Command course. One fine evening, I again went to the Officers Club with a friend. The barman looked familiar. Medium build, neatly dressed, and fair complexioned. The dark, bluish patch of skin pigmentation on his forehead was still present.

I asked him to pour us drinks. He gave me a blank look and picked up a crystal glass. A sea of itinerant trainee officers come to Mhow every year. It would be vainglorious of me to expect him to recognise me, I thought.

He picked up the bottle. He was looking at me. The light in his eyes changed, and he took out a battered old dairy from his pocket. He ruffled through the pages, went to a drawer, and took out a white envelope. He opened the envelope and kept

₹323 on the counter and said, 'Sir, you came here ten years ago and forgot to collect your balance amount.'

Then, Abid picked up the bottle and poured us our drinks. A smile of relief played on his face.

Olive Green Corduroy Trousers

The Army is often a place stiff as a *papad* with hierarchy and invisible guy ropes around the top brass. It's a nation within a nation. Perhaps it is the only real India because here, in every small set-up called a unit, there are men from all parts of the country. The human forces at play in the narrowed world of discipline, sewn by steel thread of regulations and an exasperating class system based on ranks and privilege, are forever at play. Even the length and thickness of moustaches have unwritten laws in the Army.

I remember when I got commissioned in 1966 in the Sikhs as a Second Lieutenant. My first CO was Colonel Durjan Singh from the Bikaner State Forces of the Indian Army. He was a tall, balding chap who had a bloody thick, solid moustache like a rope—a pucca Rajput of the desert.

Our battalion had just moved from Nagaland to Barrackpur near Calcutta. He commanded the battalion in full Raja style. He would come to the office at eight o'clock in the morning. Adjutant and the Subedar Major would meet and salute him.

Then, he would ask the Adjutant, 'Anything important?'

'Sir, the routine training is taking place,' the Adjutant would say. He would take the Subedar Major—a giant *sardar* built like the Zamzama cannon of Lahore.

'Come, let's go and see the training of the troops,' the CO would say, and he, along with the Adjutant and the Subedar Major, would walk out towards the battalion's training area.

As soon as they would enter the training area, he would walk two steps, notice something amiss with the first squad post of trainees, and would shout loudly from a distance, 'No *jawan*, that is not the way it is to be done. Do it properly and seriously. The enemy never gives a second chance in combat, etcetera, etcetera.'

Then he would turn back, return to his office, and call up the Adjutant.

'I am here for an hour. Get me anything you have to show me or that which requires my signatures,' the CO would announce.

The Brigade headquarters was two kilometres away from our battalion, and the CO's house was exactly two kilometres in the opposite direction of the battalion. He would get up from his chair at 10 a.m. The Subedar Major would come to him. The CO would sit in the Willys Jeep, ask the Subedar Major to get into the Jeep, and say to the driver, '*Ghar chalo.*' (Head home.)

The CO used to stay alone. His wife was in Jodhpur. He would chat with the Subedar Major for 25 minutes about what was happening in the battalion and what had to be done and give his mind to the big sardar. Then, he would tell the Subedar Major, 'Okay *sahab*, we will meet in the evening now.' And the Subedar Major would come back to the battalion.

Then, the CO would call his Batman and say, 'Fauja Singh, *sharaab lao*.' (Fauja Singh, get me a drink.)

He would open the bottle and start off his first drink of the day. At the time, our four Company Commanders were:

Major Pannu, who would have been an Army Commander had he lived. He died in the 1971 Battle of Chhamb. Lieutenant General Malhotra was the second Company Commander. The third was Major General Waseer, and the fourth Company Commander was also a hot-shot guy, Brigadier M. M. L. Ahuja, who suffered a heart attack and had a bypass surgery, or he would also have been a sure-shot General.

When I think of the past, it only tickles me, and I burst into laughter even now when I am 74 years of age. Our CO was a man of most retiring habits. Half an hour in the morning and half an hour in the evening, that's all the duration for which he appeared in the battalion. He mentored such a fine lot of officers. All four of his rifle Company Commanders became Brigadiers and Generals later on.

Not only that, our battalion used to end up winning most sports and training events of the brigade and division as well. We were part of 32 Brigade of 9 Mountain Division. We used to represent the North Bengal Sub-Area. Once, there was the Command Athletics Championship. 4 Corps Commander General Vohra came to witness the finals. His officers had told him, 'Sir, please come to receive the trophy, as 4 Corps is winning the athletics trophy straight away.'

Sam Manekshaw was the Eastern Army Commander at that time. He was the chief guest at the Command Athletics Championship. Vohra reached as anticipated and was pumped up by his staff to take the cup in the presence of Manekshaw. The whole Army knew that Manekshaw was to be the next Army Chief. Vohra also reached there to make a good impression on Manekshaw.

The final race was to be the 4x100 metres relay race on which the final result depended. Our *khalsas ragdoed* (defeated) every other team, and we were the winners. North Bengal Area had just two battalions: 5 Sikh and 19 Rajput. Two bloody, piddly battalion teams took the Eastern Command Athletics Championships Cup.

After that, we won the Eastern Command swimming championship also. That was the standard and spirit of my battalion in those days.

Our CO was a bit of a tanker as far as drinks were concerned. He took a drink at midday and took a cup now and then till sundown. Thakur *sahab*, Bikaner State Forces, red eyes, ramrod straight physique like a Rajasthani Rajput, and pointed thick moustaches—I have never seen a CO like that.

He never troubled or got behind anybody. If a *jawan* got late from leave and was marched up to him, he would gently admonish the offender, '*Jawan, tumhey sharm sey doob marna chahiye.* (Soldier, you should drown in shame.) Do not repeat it. If you repeat it, *mujhe bada afsos hoga* (I shall be disappointed), and will have to give you 28 days imprisonment as punishment. I shall also have to put you in the quarter guard.'

Then, he would address the Subedar Major once the offender had been marched out of his office, 'Subedar Major *sahab*, leave him.'

The Adjutant would interject and say, 'But, Sir, this fellow is a habitual offender. He always rejoins the battalion late and overstays his leave.'

'O Laali, give him another chance. He is a young boy and he will improve.' Laali was the name of the battalion Adjutant.

The troops used to love him. The officers used to love him even more.

Usually, the Adjutant had to remind the CO, 'Sir, you have to come to so and so place today evening to take the trophy. We are winning the football cup.'

He would turn to the Adjutant and say, '*Yaar*, you chaps are full of mischief for your old CO. You trouble me too much by winning every championship and make me attend too many podium finishes.'

He had no interest beyond the battalion. He was not interested in promotion or anything. He ran the battalion in his own style. Total *raja admi* to whom the battalion was as dear as his own family.

When our battalion was in Nagaland in counter-insurgency operations in the '60s, one Brigade Commander tried to be funny with him and tried to corner him over a very petty thing. Usually, senior officers are not bothered by small things. Brigadier K. was our new Brigade Commander. He didn't know with whom he was taking *panga*. He tried to cross swords with our Thakur *sahab* when he came for the battalion's inspection. Officers were, as is the standard practice, lined up for introduction with the Brigade Commander.

'What is this Durjan? Your bloody Captains are wearing corduroy pants. Is it authorised in dress regulations? Corduroy trousers are only authorised to Majors and above.' He hooked on to a petty technicality in the dress regulations for officers and hoped to humiliate Thakur *sahab* when he saw one of the Captains in the line wearing olive green corduroy trousers instead of the starched cotton drill trousers.

In those days, there was a great craze for olive green corduroy trousers in uniform among the officers. Only Majors and above in rank could wear them as per the prevalent dress code then.

'You have no control over your officers,' sneered the Brigadier in a superior voice that seemed to suggest, 'see how easy it is for me as a Brigade Commander to tweak your ears'.

This infuriated Thakur *sahab*. But, he was too well-bred an officer to lose his temper. It was a no-light affront to him. He said to the Brigadier, 'Sir, how is my battalion doing here in Nagaland insurgency operations?"

'Your battalion is doing very well.' And that was a fact that the Brigadier couldn't dispute. Our battalion was, in fact, doing a very good job in Nagaland.

'Sir, if my officer's efficiency is not affected by putting on a scarf or corduroy trousers, I let him put it. It is good for an officer to look neat, well-dressed and distinct. He is an officer and a leader, after all.' After a pause, he added an afterthought, 'Moreover, if tomorrow my officer will get a bullet in the chest and die, he will at least have the satisfaction that he was wearing a scarf and corduroy trousers when he stopped a bullet.'

The Brigadier was never seen again in our battalion. So, that was my first CO, Thakur Durjan Singh of Bikaner State Forces. They don't make officers like him anymore, or do they?

Book Burning

My daughter was looking at my bookcase. Some of the books were very old.

'Dad, you have some very old books here,' she said. I walked up to her. She was pointing at the faded spines of some old paperbacks.

'Oh well, those books have a little story behind them.' I smiled and started telling her about the old books and their life's journey.

'Many years ago, when I was very young, about 10 years old, we used to live in Shimla.

'Our cottage was tucked right beneath a cross-section of roads called Charing Cross. Every time a motor car or bus passed the road, the groan of the engines filled the rooms with noise. Then, the noise decreased as the vehicle passed onward. The military dispatch rider's Bullet motorcycle created the loudest racket going up Jutogh Hill on its way to the command headquarters at Shimla. The cottage received sunlight only for an hour in the morning. After that golden hour, the sun went behind the grand deodar hill on which a pretty girl lived. The house lay in the shadow of the hill, its rooms murky and dark and cold, with a fireplace in each one. When the troops of monkeys came swinging down the deodar hills, they jumped on the cottage's tin roof, and I would rush out with my catapult to chase them away.

'It was the summer break for school boys, and my older brother, who studied in a hostel near Delhi, was home.

'I heard the commotion through the open door of the drawing room as I sat making a parachute out of polythene film for my little sister, who was the cynosure of my eyes.

'Mother was clopping the older brother on his head with a book. "You miserable donkey, this is what they teach you to read in your school? This is what you have learnt? To read these filthy books? Have you seen the cover of this book? I will thrash you so much that all that you have read will fall out of your head," she had caught him reading one of father's books.

'Father had some of the saucy books of the time by writers like Harold Robbin's *Stileto*. Mother was an unlettered farm girl with decidedly fundamental Sita Mata syndrome. She shook in outrage, and her face became red in blasphemous anger. The picture of a blond European woman with a curvy bosom shined on the Fontana paperback cover. The woman in the picture was showing enough leg and bosom to make my mother think that the germs of whatever disease that picture carried had infected her son.

'"You horrible boy! Your milk teeth are yet to fall, and this is your fancy?" Her rage got self-fanned by her own cascades of curses. Mad and furious, in one fell swoop of her hands, she pulled the complete row of books to the ground from father's bookshelf.

'"I will burn all these wretched books right now!" she dragged the squirming boy by the ear and went to the kitchen to fetch the can of kerosene oil.

'I had seen the mauling my dumb brother had received. He should have had more sense than to read Harold Robbin's in front of Sita Mata's eyes. I abandoned parachute-making and placed a stone on the polythene. The books lay on the floor, waiting to be made into *Suttees*. I knew my mother's self-destructive anger too well. She carried out her threats with a primitive, adamant, rustic fury that would put Caligula to shame.

'I had warned my cuckoo older brother there would be hell to pay for if mother caught him reading the forbidden books on father's bookshelf. But he was lazy and headless.

'Time was ticking fast. I ran to the slaughter site and hurriedly made a pile of the dark, shiny paperbacks that needed to be saved from the book *suttee* that would soon take place. Hans Helmuth Kirst's *The Revolt of Gunner Asch* looked covetous—with a lopsided grin at the curvy bosom of a Frau sitting in night undress from the cover of yet another Fontana paperback. I heard my mother's footsteps returning. Swiftly and silently, like a burglar, I slipped out of the rear door to the coal shed in the backyard. I had saved a few books, but not all.

'It was my job in the house to break the large coal rocks that came as fuel for heating with a hammer and hack wood for the fireplaces of the house. There was a fireplace in each room of the cottage. There was a lot of coal and blocks of wood in the shed. I dug a hole in the heap of black anthracite, covered up the books in a gunny sack, and hid them in the coal. I was sure mother wouldn't find them there. She threw the rest of the books on the lawn, poured kerosene oil on them, and burnt them.

'That's how I saved those Hans Helmutt Kirst novels when I was about your age,' I said, pointing to the older books. My wife stood at the dinner table, and my daughter sat having a pre-dinner cookie and listening to my story.

The daughter got up, dusted her hands, and said blithely, 'Papa, there are too many books in our house. The first thing that I will do when you die is to make a bonfire and burn all your books.' I couldn't help ruing the fact that she had her grandmother's genes.

The Lost Shoe

~

In India, news spreads fast, like the winds carrying the monsoon rains. And bad news travels the fastest.

An ash cloud of horror fell out of the sky upon our village, and the same hushed words passed from lip to lip.

'*Ladakh mein 5 Jat khatam ho gaye.*' (The 5th battalion of the Jat Regiment has been destroyed in Ladakh.) The news was such that people felt electrocuted, as if a high voltage of shock had entered their being.

Old women sat over their urns of milk and slowly pulled the toggle cords listlessly to make butter and wept silent tears at the news. Those young men who used to come home every year bearing news of far-off lands, telling them how the rest of the world outside was, would never be seen again. The pride of their homes, and the life breath of their parents. Feeble were the hands doing work, as if blood had leaked from their veins.

They collected and came to assuage my grandmother. They said good words of honour and recounted the boy's gentle memories, his affable memories starting from childhood, for in our village, the character is an open book. Deeds are registered from the first nascent steps and live like a testament in the book of commonplace memories of the close-knit community.

Of what benefit are the balms of others to a mother, a widow who had, by dint of extraordinary and superhuman grit, brought her kids through Partition and struggled, cutting her way through the forest of trouble? That is a poor widow's daily life.

'It cannot be true!' she roared like a lioness, broken, shaking her fists to the heavens. 'First, the Gods take my man, and now my son!' she raged and raged. Her earth had shifted its equator, and her universe had left its steady revolutions. The anger of that woman's unjust fate shook the throne of the Gods in heaven.

She refused to believe anybody. The world could disintegrate, but her child was hers, and not even the Gods had the right to take him away from her. He is, and will always be, exclusively hers alone. No, the Gods or anyone cannot take him, he—who is not theirs, but hers alone.

When she arrived in my maternal grandfather's village, my mother, who saw my grandmother that day, narrated the scene to me.

'*Thaari daadi ney kurta ulta pehan rakhya thaa, arr ek paon me jutti nahi thee, arr aankh katee laal thee.*' (She was wearing her shirt inside out, was missing a shoe, and her eyes were red like blood.)

My maternal grandfather had been an emergency commissioned officer during the British Raj days. He calmed my grandmother, '*Chowdhran, key baat ho gayi?*' (Chowdhran, what's the matter?)

'*Meraa laal, Mewa khatam ho gaya,*' (My beloved son, Mewa has perished) she waited.

'It's just a rumour,' my maternal grandfather assured her. 'Many rumours fly during war times. Sometimes, even telegrams carry the wrong news. Let's not lose hope,' he told her. Then, he thought what he should do. He had also heard the news of 5 Jat being mauled in the war going on in the Himalayan ranges.

'I will leave for Army Headquarters right now and get some news. You stop worrying your head off. What have you made of yourself? *Himmat rakh, Chowdhran.*' (Stay strong, Chowdhran.)

A kindly officer attended the white-turbanned old veteran in Army Headquarters in Delhi, '*Tauji*, it's very difficult to ascertain the fate of your boy. But I will try. Come tomorrow.'

The old man went and slept under an old tree and presented himself the next day to the officer.

The officer told him to wait, and he waited the whole day. No results came forth. He again went and slept under a tree, and presented himself the next day.

After four days, he was rewarded with the news that the soldier he had come looking for lived and was well.

My maternal grandfather came back to the village with the glad tidings. And my grandmother, who had not touched a morsel of food all these days, ate a chappati and wore her garments the proper way, and someone gave her an old *jutti* to replace the one she had lost.

About Fauji Days

Our faujis are the nation's lifeline, and their culture, traditions, and history are our proud heritage.

Fauji Days is a unique oral history initiative launched to cherish and celebrate this heritage through interviews and recordings since Faujis always have tons of inspiring, thought-provoking, funny, or engaging stories to tell.

Fauji Days has also published over numerous military books. www.faujidays.com features blogs, reference, and archival material, and a community newsletter you can subscribe.

We welcome you to be a part of Fauji Days, no matter what color uniform you wore or whether you served on terra firma, flew in the air, or rode the waves.

Your contributions to this archive of India's valor can be in the form of interviews, recordings, books, nostalgic pieces, anecdotes, pictures, or any other content you may wish to share with the wider community.

All we want is to know your story, so that India knows her story better. It is incomplete without yours.

Jai Hind!

Fauji Days Oral History

More From Fauji Days

Military Pensions Simplified:
Commentary, Case Law & Provisions
Navdeep Singh
ISBN: 978-93-92210-06-8

Gyan Chakra on India's Military Strategy
Edited by Major General Amarjit Singh
ISBN: 978-93-92210-18-1

The Crossover Girl & Other Stories
Ashok Ahlawat
ISBN: 978-93-92210-22-8

Pick of the Army: Guns, Gunners and Mules
The Indian Mountain Artillery, 1851–1985
Lieutenant General NS Brar
ISBN: 978-93-92210-20-4

Drummers Call:
An Anthology of Writings While Following the Drum
Lieutenant General NS Brar
ISBN: 978-93-88150-00-2

Engineering the Victory March:
Bangladesh Liberation War 1971
Brigadier RB Singh
ISBN: 978-93-92210-03-7

The General Called Tsunami: Memoir of a Sapper
Lieutenant General BS Dhaliwal
ISBN: 978-93-92210-05-1

The POW Who Saved Kashmir:
Unsung Saga of Sher Bachha Brig Pritam Singh, MC
Brigadier Jasbir Singh and Pankaj P Singh
ISBN: 978-93-88150-04-0

Dusk over the Mustard Fields
Ranjit Powar
ISBN: 978-93-92210-21-1

Fauji Days Classics

On War
General Carl Von Clausevitz
ISBN: 978-93-92210-13-6

Hira Singh
Talbot Mundy
ISBN: 978-93-92210-09-9

Generals Die in Bed
Charles Yale Harrison
ISBN: 978-93-92210-44-0

Three Soldiers
John Dos Passos
ISBN: 978-93-92210-14-3

War Is a Racket
Smedley D Butler
ISBN: 978-93-92210-15-0

The Red Badge of Courage
Stephen Crane
ISBN: 978-93-92210-16-7

Other Titles From The Browser

Ekarat: Stories He Left Behind
ISBN: 978-93-92210-08-2

Mahroks: The Story of the Kambojas, Sikhs and Shaheeds
Jewan Deepak
ISBN: 978-93-5737-645-7

The Nightingale and Other Stories
Maniki Deep
ISBN: 978-81-94954-27-9

In and Out of Step
GS Aujla, IPS (Retd)
ISBN: 978-93-88150-17-0

Sociopreneur: Zero to One
Kunal Nandwani
ISBN: 978-93-88150-11-8

Wilderness Is Us: Hiking, Thriving and Learning in the Great Outdoors
Vipul Negi
ISBN: 978-93-88150-07-1